# It All Began on Kennerly Street

D1523272

SHARON ROWLAND

PAGE PUBLISHING, INC.
Conneaut Lake, PA

First originally published by Page Publishing 2020

ISBN 978-1-6624-1319-3 (pbk)
ISBN 978-1-6624-1320-9 (digital)

Printed in the United States of America

Mama, throughout the years, you have shared various stories about your life, and they have colored and shaped my world in such a way that it has inspired me to write this book dedicated to your memory. You will forever be in my heart, and I will carry you with me always.

Your loving daughter,
Sharon

# *Let Me Tell You About My Mama*

She wiped my tears, kissed my wounds, and held on to my hand.

She visited me at my hospital bed for weeks until I was able to stand.

She laid my head on her chest and gave comfort to me.

She told me, "Things will get better, baby, you just wait and see."

She smiled and was strong for me even though she had her own pain.

She protected and covered me with her prayers—they were never in vain.

She reminded me of my greatness and self-worth.

She taught me about the love of God and raised me in the church.

She opened her doors to give shelter and let people in.

She cooked for us all: family, church members, coworkers, and friends.

She celebrated and encouraged me; she gave me honest advice.

She was a great storyteller, her stories laced with humor and sprinkled with lessons about life.

She saw the real me when I was being illusory and trying my best to hide.

She would patiently wait for me to "get over it" when we didn't see eye to eye.

She taught me how to act like a lady and exhibit dignity and grace.

She fixed my hair and clothes whenever something was out of place.

She was my mother, my biggest fan and my best friend.

She loved me unconditionally, right to the very end.

I know she's up in heaven watching over me even now.

I'll cherish the memories until I see her again—until then, I'll carry on. Somehow.

Dear Lord, I hope that I can be half the woman she was.

And that I might touch others with the same generosity and love.

# PREFACE

This story is based on the true life events of my mother, Dorothy Elizabeth Rowland. Names and certain details have been changed to protect the privacy of the individuals who were a part of her story. I also added a fictional character named Aurora—who appears in the story as a hospital patient sitter. This character is simply a component of dramatic interpretation. She represents the guardian angels that I personally believe are assigned to us by God.

Also, within my writing, I wanted to give breath to the many stories my mother would often share about her life growing up in St. Louis, Missouri, with her siblings, and her many accounts of things that happened to her as an adult. She often would talk about the fun and exciting times she has had throughout her life walk—from the good ole days of apartment management, to the flamboyant characters at her work, to the many memorable interactions with family, friends, and church members.

Although this book was mainly written for personal therapeutic purposes, it was also written for entertainment purposes as well. But it is my hope that the reader will walk away from it motivated to live their life in such a way that when it's all said and done, their life story will be spoken well of and shared by others, inspiring future generations of storytellers. We all have millions of moments in life that we record and store in the recesses of our minds. These moments shape who we are and give spark to who we can become.

CHAPTER ONE

# *Tell Me About You!*

I'm eighty-four years old, and this is what it has come to? How did I end up lying here in this hospital bed? I thought I just came here for a few tests! No one even realizes I can hear them talking over me. My daughter, Sheryl, is here to see me this morning, and my heart is leaping with love for her. No matter how old she gets, she's always going to be my baby girl. Maybe she came to take me home.

My head is pounding, and for some reason, all I can do is mumble a word or two—my strength is just about gone. I remember that before I came here, the last few days at home were really rough. She was so worried about me. I could see it in her eyes. She takes such good care of me, but things are getting to be a bit difficult lately.

Sometimes I hear noises around the house whenever she's gone, so I don't like it much when she goes out. I don't want to hold her hostage, but whenever she's home, I feel so much better. So, I'm sure that once I get out of this hospital and go home, I'll be all right. I'm sure this is nothing that a little pain medicine and prayer can't fix.

I'm so glad Sheryl is here. I wanna tell her about how somebody sat at my bedside all night last night. I couldn't really make out who it was, a lady, I think, but she sat here just as quiet as you please. I felt an indescribable sense of peace over me the whole time she was here. A subtle glow surrounded her as she sat by my bed. At some point, I drifted off to sleep but woke back up. I looked to my right to see if she was still there… Yep, the kind stranger never left my side. I know one thing, if she comes back before I leave, I'm going to try my best to find out who she is and thank her for taking the time to sit with me. But now my baby girl is here to keep me company.

"Mama…Mama, can you hear me? I love you, Mama."

"I love you…" I mumble in response.

The pain in my head is almost unbearable. I want to say more to her, but I simply can't get it out. She's taken my hands and is cupping them in hers and holding them up to her cheek. I can feel the wetness on her face, and I realize that she is silently crying. I want to wipe her tears, but I can't coordinate my movements. All I can do is moan and fiddle my hands. I hate to see her upset, but I'm not able to comfort her. She lets go of my hands and plants a warm kiss on my forehead then makes her way to the chair to the right of my bed. I'm so tired. I'll just rest my eyes…

I must've drifted off to sleep because now the room is full of family. My two sons, Joshua Jr. and Darryl, are also here and my grandkids. And I see a few other familiar faces from church. I wonder what all these folks are doing here. This must be pretty serious if all of them have come to see me. Lord, have mercy! Sweet Jesus! What's wrong with me?

Oh, wait. Now a doctor has entered the room and is pulling Sheryl to the side. I can't really make out what he's telling her with all the others in the room talking and standing over me. I want to yell, "Would y'all please shut up so I can hear what they're saying!" But my mouth doesn't want to work right! And now here's the nurse joining them. Okay, she's making her way over here by me. But I can't even muster up enough strength to ask her what's going on. I see she's putting something in my IV. Oh my goodness…I feel so drowsy I can't keep my eyes open…

I'm awake again. The room is dark and silent now. I feel a warm sensation on my right side. So, I slowly turn my head, and there she is again! My unknown visitor! I have to at least try to say hello and find out who she is. But before I can say anything, she's greeting me.

"Hello, Elizabeth. Everyone else has gone home now. But don't worry, you'll be out of here very soon."

The mystery lady looks to be about thirty or so, with a slim build. She has a very warm smile and eyes to match. I feel like I know her from somewhere, but I can't make it out in my head from where. I just know that she seems familiar to me. I don't want to be rude and just lie here silent, but I can't do anything but mumble.

Funny thing is, I'm not much of a conversationalist anyway, I don't really engage in small talk. But everybody who knows me knows that when I'm in the mood, I usually have a good story or two to share. Heck, I've always got good stories to tell. And most people love it when I tell 'em. Whether it's when we're all sitting around after a large family dinner or if it's just me and one lone soul who's willing and ready for a good laugh! I always said that I could write a book about my life. It has certainly been an interesting one, to say the least.

Again, I try to say something to her, but my words just aren't coming out.

"Elizabeth, I'll be here with you every night until you leave this place, so don't worry. And we'll have plenty of time to get to know each other. Just rest for now, and maybe later on you can tell me about yourself. Something tells me you might have a few interesting things you could share about yourself."

I nod my head, smile, and drift back off to sleep. For how long, I don't know. It seems like I've been out for quite a while. But now that I'm awake yet again, I feel unbelievably rested. So much so that I think I have the energy now to finally say a few words to my visitor.

She smiles at me and says, "Hello, Elizabeth. It looks like you're feeling a little better, huh? I'm going to be here with you for the rest of the night, so maybe you can tell me a little bit about yourself. We've got nothing but time."

Surprisingly, I'm now able to speak clearly. That knockout medicine that the nurse put in my IV must've worn off.

I shift my focus toward my visitor. "Hello. Do you mind telling me your name and why you've been sitting at my bedside these past two nights?"

"Well, my name is Aurora, and let's just say it's a part of my duty to sit by your side and keep you company."

"Oh…well, that explains it. So, you're like a patient sitter here at the hospital, huh?"

Smiling again and nodding, she says, "Yes, something like that."

"Well, it's nice to meet you, Aurora. So, you say you want me to tell you about myself. Well, let's see." Knowing I have already prepared a couple of things in my mind to share, I continue. "Well, some people might say I'm somewhat feisty, and I've even been told that I'm a bit…"

She interrupts me. "No, Elizabeth, I want to hear *your* story. Not what others might've said. Tell me about what makes you, well, you. I want to hear Elizabeth's story." She settles back in the chair and folds her arms, smiles yet again and says, "And please start from the beginning, my dear. Because as I've said before, we've got nothing but time."

I smile back and say, "Okay…okay…"

*****

I was born in St. Louis, Missouri, in 1931. My earliest memories are of the time when I had to be about three or four years old. On a typical day, music from an old out-of-tune piano could be heard pouring out the windows of our little shotgun house on Kennerly Street. It sounded like a good ole Pentecostal praise session accompanied by children's laughter and dancing. My mother sat at the piano, striking the keys as if she were in a full-fledged gospel concert. Every few minutes, she'd turn her head slightly left to sneak a peek at me and my brothers and sisters while we pretended to be dancing a "holy ghost jig."

We loved to imitate the sanctified folks down at the church because this was pretty much all we knew. Six days a week, there was always something going on down at Kennedy Temple Church of God in Christ (COGIC), and nine times out of ten, all the members of my family were right there participating in whatever was going on. Tuesday night was adult choir rehearsal. Wednesday night was Bible study. Thursday night, youth choir rehearsal. Friday night, members' meeting. Saturday was the Sunshine Band Children's Ministry. Then on Sunday, we had Sunday school at 8:00 a.m., followed by the morning service at 10:00 a.m., followed by evening service at 4:00

p.m., which usually lasted until 7:00 p.m., or longer if the spirit was high.

Going to the house of the Lord was a true way of life for us, and growing up COGIC came with high expectations. My father and mother, Carl and Mildred Davidson, were simply determined that their children would be raised with fear of the Lord in their hearts.

There was a lot of love among this Davidson clan, but there was also a great deal of discipline within my parents' household as well. My father was a God-fearing man who went to work every day while my mother stayed at home and cared for us children. My mother was a beautiful, full-figured woman, with smooth caramel-colored skin and the prettiest set of legs west of the St. Louis Municipal Bridge. Dad loved her with all his heart but didn't quite know how to show it. It was very obvious that they had no problem with intimacy in the bedroom, proven by the steady and consistent stream of Davidson babies being born. A child every year to be exact.

My oldest brother, Walter, was born from my mom's first marriage. Her first husband passed away after the fifth year of their union. Not long after that, she met and married our dad and had six additional children.

First to be born after Walter was Carl Jr. He was so handsome and charming, and he looked just like our dad. Then there was Myrtle. She was the super smart one out of the group. But along with brains, she also had beauty. She was a perfect mixture of our mom and dad. After her came Gregory. He was the most rambunctious of us all. He was always getting into some kind of trouble, but he had a heart of gold. Then there's me, Elizabeth. I was the protector of my siblings. I took care of them all, and I would literally kill a bear if it tried to harm any of my sisters or brothers! After me came Donald. He was the super religious one and superstrong! I mean really physically strong! Anything we needed done that required brute strength, we'd call on Donald, and he'd get it done, and most times all by himself. Last was our baby sister, Doris. She was the prim and proper one. Although there were a few years between her and Myrtle, they would often be mistaken for twins.

Now although that little two-bedroom shotgun home was bursting at the seams, there was a little girl in the neighborhood who my mother had taken in and loved as if she was her own. Judith was her name, and she fit right in with our Davidson clan. Judith was a sassy, petite little thing. She could talk more trash than a little bit and didn't bite her tongue for nobody. We all knew that we had a special bond, and nothing and no one could break it.

Most days while living on Kennerly, life was pretty normal. Just us being kids. One day when I was about four years old, my brother Donald bet me that I couldn't do a cartwheel through what was a broken off part of the front porch railing and land on my feet in the grass. I thought to myself that this ought to be an easy bet to win because I could do cartwheels in my sleep. So, I took the bet! I was small enough that I could certainly clear and go straight through the opening in the railing with no problem. But little did I know that there was an old broken umbrella leaning up against the foot of the porch.

A sharp piece of metal from the umbrella was sticking up just high enough right where my head would need to clear the porch. As I was upside down midway through the railing, my face hit the metal, and it cut through my flesh just above my right eye. Blood was gushing everywhere! Donald was screaming so loud that it startled my mother who was up on a chair washing the windows on the front of the house.

She swung around and jumped down off the chair and scooped me up in her arms. I know she wasn't thinking because she took the dirty old washrag that she was using to clean the windows and held it over my eye, trying to stop the blood from pouring out. She ran with me to Dr. Ferguson's house. He was a medical doctor who lived directly across the street from us. He probably was the only black doctor in our area of town, and thankfully, he lived so close because it seemed that we, Davidson children, were always getting hurt doing something or other.

Mama had me cupped up in one arm while she banged wildly on Dr. Ferguson's front door with the other. She was yelling, I was crying, and poor Donald was standing on our porch screaming! I'm sure Donald was just as terrified and traumatized as I was. Finally, Dr. Ferguson flung open the door and came rushing out.

Mama handed me to him. "Please, Dr. Ferguson! Can you help my baby? She cut herself falling off the porch. Please! She's bleeding so badly. I can't get it to stop!"

"Let's bring her inside. I'll take a look at her."

Well, all I remember afterward is that after he got the bleeding to stop, I had to get stitches, and I had to wear a big ole patch above my eye to cover up my wound. I remember going around to each of my brothers and sisters and showing off my big white patch with pride.

I seemed to always be getting into some kind of trouble with Donald. I remember one day, not too long after the cartwheel incident, we were both playing in the street in front of the house, and Donald, being as strong as he was, was able to lift up the heavy sewer grate next to the curb. And for some crazy reason, I wanted to help him. I slipped my tiny little fingers right next to his to help hold it up, but Donald let go and the grate came slamming down on the tip of my left middle finger, and it took a piece of the meaty side of my finger with it. Once again, there we were screaming and crying in unison. I know we probably drove my mother crazy with all the things we found ourselves getting into. She never really showed signs of being tired, but I know that she had to be worn-out having a total of eight children to contend with.

Whippings usually got handed out by our father. If one of us did something wrong, the others didn't want to tell. And because of that, he'd line us all up in a row and let us know that he was going to whip us all if no one 'fessed up to the wrongdoing. Donald would more often than not burst out crying, praying and calling on the name of Jesus so loud that you would've thought he was an old Baptist preacher. But that didn't deter Daddy at all. He would tear into all our hides so tough until he got tired.

During the warmer days of the year, we often stayed outside in an effort to stay out of our father's way. And for there being so many of us, we usually played together very well. I honestly don't recall us ever getting into any major disputes. Our oldest brother, Walter, was seven years older than Carl Jr., and so he typically was the one who managed us all while we played. I believe he either took his job too seriously or he just thought it was funny to stop us dead in our tracks every ten or fifteen minutes and make us stand still while he counted us to make sure we were all present and accounted for.

He'd start from the youngest on up. "One, two, three, four…let me see…five, six, seven. Yep. You're all here."

Carl Jr. would get so irritated with him. "Hey, man, you don't have to count me. I'm old enough to take care of myself. I'm not a baby."

Carl Jr. was usually quiet, but every once in a while, if something got next to him bad enough, he'd definitely let it be known. But Walter ain't pay him no mind. He just went right back to doing whatever it was he was doing until the next moment when he felt like it was time to stop everything and count us again.

Next door to us was a little boy named Leroy. Leroy had what some would consider to be very effeminate qualities. He was about six years old and was more of a dainty flower than any of us girls. Leroy liked to play with the girls more than he did the boys. But at that age, none of us really cared how Leroy acted. We girls just wanted him to play "house" with us and help make the mud pies we were going to serve our imaginary family.

We needed him as our source of water to mix with the dirt in order to make the pies. Leroy always seemed to have a bladder full of water, enough to make at least three good-size mud pies. He'd stand right there in the dirt, unfasten his pants, take aim, and let the water flow. We girls stood back so we wouldn't get splattered by the mud.

Then Leroy would help us pat down the pies and shape them until they were a perfect circle. Now how nasty was that? I can chuckle about it now. Hahaha… Yes, Lord, Leroy was one of our best playmates.

As children, because of my parents' religious beliefs, we weren't allowed to go swimming, play sports, listen to the radio, or anything like that. We did, however, have a pair of roller skates that some of us took turns using. And our father also helped us build our very own soapbox cart. This was like what we call a go-kart nowadays but without an engine. It used gravity, you see…so we would have to start at the top of the hill on our street, jump in, and steer our way all the way down to the bottom of the hill. We absolutely loved that soapbox cart! We must've played with that thing from sunup to sundown every day of the summer months. But on rainy days, we all would have to be cooped up in that little shotgun house.

On one particular rainy day, there was a knock at the front door. It was Sister Middleton. She was one of the members down at the church and a good friend to our mother. Now Sister Middleton had an enormous backside. It was like a coffee table. It stuck out just as far and wide as the great outdoors! And it would jiggle and bounce up and down despite the girdle she was wearing.

As a matter of fact, I think that girdle she wore faithfully every day may not have ever seen the likes of any water or washing powder. I say this because Sister Middleton had an odor that introduced her as she entered a room and lingered behind to bid a disrespectful fare-well as she exited. It was so bad that it was the biggest thing us kids talked and giggled about, aside from the atrociousness of her giant rumble seat.

She loved to make a grand entrance whenever she came over. Mama would open the door and in sashayed Sister Middleton, wear-ing her canary, yellow, floral print dress, with a white pocketbook and white gloves. She'd hang her pocketbook over her left arm and hold her right hand in the air, slightly bent at the wrist, as if she was the queen of England. She walked right past us and made her way to her favorite chair in the house. Now that I think about it, it probably was her favorite chair because it was the only one that she could fit into without getting stuck.

But one thing I can say about Sister Middleton is she had an absolutely beautiful voice. She could sing like nobody's business. And with her singing and Mama's piano playing, we would have a good ole time right there in the front room of our house.

After sitting a spell, singing, laughing and drinking tea, it was about time for Sister Middleton to head on home. She'd call one of my brothers over to help pull her up out of the chair—most times Donald because he was the strongest. Then she'd stand there a few seconds to let her joints get primed and prepared so she could sashay her way on out the door. And so it was, she left in just as grand fashion as when she came.

When Mama let her out and retired to the back of the house, my siblings and I would start giggling and snickering as we held our noses saying, "Ewwww! She smells."

Then for the life of me, I can't tell you why, but we'd all take turns bending down to take a good whiff of the seat where Sister Middleton had sat, giggling and pinching our noses, saying, "Ewwww, it stinks!" Ha ha! Lord, have mercy, I don't know why we did that! Just plain silly, I guess.

The days of my childhood were very eventful. If I wasn't playing with our dog, Roscoe, I was playing with my siblings. And if I wasn't playing with my siblings, I was defending them against some neighborhood child who was trying to harm them. I could fight. Yes, I could fight better than any boy. I was a stocky child. I guess I took after my mother in that respect. I was taller and bigger than my other two sisters, I was bolder than any of my brothers, and I had just as much spunk, if not more, than our bonus little sister, Judith. I wasn't afraid of anybody! I wasn't a bully, nah... You see, I just wasn't gonna let no one run over me or anyone I cared about.

When I was about seven years old, there was one certain girl in our neighborhood. I can't remember her name, but she was a real bruiser. She used to catch the kids who walked home from school and beat them up and take whatever they had that she wanted. Well, one day, she caught me walking home from school and decided that she was going to start in with me. That was probably the worst decision she ever could have made.

As I walked past her, she pushed me in my back and said, "Hey, fat girl."

I turned around and asked her to repeat what she said.

She said it again, "I said, 'Hey, fat girl!'"

Then she hauled off and hit me dead in my face. I reacted so fast I didn't even realize that I had grabbed her by one of her braided ponytails and pulled her down to the ground. I continued to hold on to that braid and dragged her several feet in the dirt and rocks. Then I straddled her and started hitting her in her face.

By the time I was done with her, my brother, Gregory, was yelling, "Elizabeth! Stop! Get off that girl!"

I snapped to and realized what I was doing, so I got up and stood over her while she was screaming and crying. I looked down at my right hand and realized that I was still holding her little braided ponytail clenched tightly in my fist. I looked at it and dropped it right next to her while she was sitting there in the dirt crying and rocking while holding her bloody knees.

By this time, the other kids had run over to witness what happened, and I dusted myself off and slowly but proudly walked away. I smiled all the way home. But I was unaware of what awaited me once I got there.

I walked up onto the porch and slowly opened the front door, peeking inside to see if I could spy my mother anywhere. I didn't want her to be upset with me for dirtying up my dress. I tiptoed past the front room, which also served as the bedroom for us girls. I tiptoed down the hall and headed toward my brothers' bedroom to remove my dress, change into another, and head out back to rinse out the dirt stains in my dress in the old tin tub on the back porch. But before I could get to the back room, my brother, Walter, called my name.

"Elizabeth!" I turned and looked at him and saw sadness in his eyes. "Mama isn't doing too well, so y'all keep it down today."

I nodded and continued toward the back. Once I finished hand cleaning stains out of my dress, I returned through the back door and tiptoed toward my parents' bedroom. I peeked around the door and saw my father standing over my mother, holding her hand and praying.

I had never seen my mother lying down during the middle of the day, so I figured that she must've been sick and needed the rest. But the way Daddy was praying made me wonder if it was something more serious than just a stomachache or headache. Two days later, Mama was gone…leaving behind a crop of small kids and a broken-hearted husband to try to make it without her.

To this day, I'm not sure what it was that caused our mother's death. We were such little kids, so I guess my father, or the other adults in our lives, didn't think to sit us down and talk to us about it. After I got grown, I figured that it might've been a stroke or heart attack, not sure. Or maybe her body just wasn't able to properly heal after having a child every year for six years straight. I don't know. All I know is, our lives weren't ever the same after our mother passed. Not ever.

# Black-Ass Nellie

It had been a little over a year since our mother had passed. Judith continued to stay with us until her aunt (her mother's sister) moved into a house very close by us. This allowed her to care for Judith and for us to continue to have her in our lives as our sister.

By this time, Walter was age eighteen and had moved out and on with his life. The rest of us were all pretty much just going through the motions. We were all school age, ranging from age six on up to age eleven, and thankfully our father was able to keep us all under his care.

Everyone had to pitch in and help out Daddy. When it came to what needed to be done around the house, the girls did the cleaning, the boys did the outside chores, and our father did the cooking. He was an excellent cook, and he seemed to love doing it. I guess it was a healthy distraction from him just sitting in his room and staring at the walls, thinking about Mama.

One Saturday morning, Daddy got up extra early and started fiddling around in the kitchen. He was picking and cleaning greens, frying chicken in the big cast-iron skillet, stirring and mixing up a cake, and Lord knows what else he had going on in there. We kids were getting ready to head out the door for the Sunshine Band Children's Ministry down at the church.

As we were leaving out the door, Daddy yelled out to tell us, "Y'all be home by three o'clock because we got company coming over and I want y'all back home in time."

We all yelled back in unison as if we were singing, "Okay, Dad-deeeee!"

I figured it must be somebody real important if he was doing all this cooking on a Saturday. This type of spread was usually reserved for dinner after church on Sundays. Whoever it was that was coming must be a relative from out of town or something. In any case, it didn't really matter to me who it was, I just couldn't wait to get back home so I could eat all what my father was cooking!

By one o'clock, we all had made it back from church and were sitting patiently, waiting for our guest to arrive. Right at three o'clock, there was a knock at the door. My little sister, Doris, jumped down off the sofa and ran to the door. I looked up and saw her just standing there gazing at somebody outside. I got up to go see who it was, and I froze in my tracks too. I heard Daddy yelling from the kitchen to let our guests in. I slowly pushed open the screen door and let them in. I couldn't believe it. It was Sister Nellie Coltrane and her daughter, Wendy. I was thinking, *What are they doing here?*

Wendy was about seventeen years old. She had the finest clothes out of anyone I knew. And today she was wearing a beautiful, royal blue, A-line coat with big white buttons all the way down the front. Her mother was a seamstress and could make almost anything with a needle and thread. I loved that coat and wished that I could have one just like Wendy's. Wendy smiled at me with a devilish little smirk as she walked right past me and Doris into our living room. She didn't speak, and neither did we.

Her mother, Nellie, was a tall, dark-skinned woman, her complexion the color of a cup of deep roast coffee, smooth and rich. She also had big, round, bright eyes. They were so big that she looked like she was surprised all the time.

"Hello, little ones," she said as she scooted past me and Doris.

She stood there in our front room panting hard, like she had just run all the way to our house.

"Lord, it's so cold out there. And that wind! Whew! That wind near 'bout blew me right over!"

She was talking to us like we really cared anything about what she was saying. One of the many things I disliked about Nellie was that she was always putting on airs and acting like she was a better person than she really was. I couldn't help but think about all the times she would be in church skinnin' and grinnin' at my father after my mother died. She was doing it well before my mother had passed, but she was way more obvious with it now. However, she never paid us kids no mind unless she was shooting us evil looks during service if she felt like we were getting a little too noisy. She was an usher at the church and was one of the sternest ones there.

My father yelled out from the kitchen, "Hello, ladies! Come on in and rest your feet."

He then started making his way to the front room. He was holding a dish towel and drying his hands, and he smiled at Nellie and Wendy. He motioned for me to move closer to them.

"Elizabeth, don't just stand there. Take their wraps."

I moved closer to them and held my arms straight out for them to lay their coats across. Wendy laid her coat across my arms nice and neatly, in such a fashion as to let me know that she wanted me to take great care with it. Her mother, Nellie, on the other hand, tossed her coat so freely that it nearly covered my entire head.

I slowly walked to the back bedroom, barely able to see, and laid their coats across my father's bed. I stood there for what felt like forever, thinking about my mother and how much I missed her. I was also wondering if my father planned that dinner in an effort to win us over to the idea of Nellie becoming a part of our family. The thought of it made me sick inside. To imagine her being in our home every day was just too much to consider. Having Nellie replace my mother as my stepmother would be the worst thing that could ever happen to me, so I thought.

We all had dinner together that night. No one really said much. We all just sat there, eating and looking down at our plates, every so often I would steal a look at my father. He was grinning at Nellie like a Cheshire cat, and she seemed to be loving every minute of it. I felt nauseated and wanted to get up and storm out, but I knew my daddy would tear into my hide if I did. So, I sat there swallowing my feelings right along with the fried chicken.

Three months later, Daddy married Nellie. Both she and Wendy moved in, and just as I had feared, things only got worse. Nellie started out trying to be cordial to us all, but she couldn't keep up the charade for long. Not more than two weeks of being there, she started to show us her true colors. But when our father got home, it was a whole different act. I remember how she would make us clean up behind her and Wendy, on top of our regular chores.

One day, Wendy came home from being out and was complaining about not feeling well. She had been on her menstrual. Back then, we didn't have the normal feminine products we have now. Wendy was using large cloth baby diapers while she was menstruating. She came straight into the house and went into the back bedroom where Nellie was, and I could hear them whispering.

Then I heard Nellie say, "I'll get Myrtle to do it. You just lay down right here on the bed, and I'll bring you something warm to drink to help with your cramps. Myrtle! Come here."

Myrtle, who was ten years old at the time, was sitting in the big chair by the piano, curled up reading a book. She slammed the book shut, rolled her eyes, and let out a big sigh. "What does she want now?" she mumbled as she made her way to the back.

"Go outside and get that tin tub and put it on the back porch. Then I want you to get a big pot of water and put it on the stove and warm it up. Take that water, pour it in the tub, and put some washing powder in there. Wendy's got some used menstrual rags that need washing out. Let 'em soak for a while, then they'll need a good scrubbing to get 'em clean. Then you need to hang them up to dry… Do you hear me? Myrtle! You heard me! Get going!"

Myrtle didn't say anything in response. She just did as she was told, but I could see that there was something stirring in her, a pressure building that would soon explode.

Wendy was always treated like a princess. She didn't have to lift a finger. All she would do was go whispering to her mother, and then came the list of things we had to do that should've been Wendy's to do. In addition to that, Nellie would rub it in our faces that she was our "mother" now and there wasn't anything any one of us could do to change that. In all actuality, she wasn't a good mother at all. Hell, she wasn't a good anything! She was mean, she was lazy, she couldn't cook, and she certainly didn't show us any form of love. As a matter of fact, she did just the opposite. She made us do all the work while she sat there drinking a tall glass of whatever and barking out orders to us.

We had a big chifforobe cabinet that we used as a pantry for the food that didn't need to be kept in the icebox. Nellie would take the key to that cabinet and lock it all day so that we couldn't get anything to eat until right before Daddy came home. About fifteen minutes before it was time for him to get home, Nellie would unlock the cabinet, go to her bedroom, tie her hair up in a scarf, jump into the bed, and pull the covers all the way up to her big bubbled eyes. She did this because she wanted Daddy to think she had done all the housework and was now resting because she was tired. This was a daily ritual of hers. By the time I was twelve years old, I'd had enough of her treating us like servants.

One day during the summer months, our father had just left out the door for work, and Wendy was out as well. Nellie started walking around the house, complaining and telling us to get up and get to cleaning. Well, I couldn't take it anymore, so I went into the kitchen and grabbed the biggest knife I could find, and before she could get to that pantry cabinet key, I had taken it.

I walked up to Nellie, holding the knife straight out, pointed it dead at her face, and said, "Why don't you take yo' black ass back to bed and leave us alone!"

She was holding up her hands, and I could tell that she was in shock. "Elizabeth! What the hell are you doing?"

I took a step toward her and backed her up into her bedroom. "I'm fixing to carve you from head to toe, if you don't leave us alone!"

She was shaking like a leaf. She scurried backward into her bedroom and slammed the door. "They said you was crazy, and now I believe it!"

"Yeah, and I'm crazy enough to do just what I said if you come back out here!"

I stayed posted at that door all day, holding that knife, while my brothers and sisters got the pantry cabinet key from me, and we all sat right there in the hallway outside Nellie's door and ate just as much food as we pleased. Needless to say, Nellie didn't try to come out of that bedroom all day. And about ten minutes before it was time for Daddy to get home from work, in that same disingenuous fashion as Nellie usually did each day, I put the pantry key back in its place, put the knife back in the kitchen, and took a seat on the sofa right next to Myrtle and Doris. The boys went outside to play, and things felt right for the first time in a long time.

Another two years had passed, and by this time, Wendy had moved out and was married. It was graduation time for my sister, Myrtle, who was now sixteen, and she needed a new dress. The one and only thing Nellie could do well was sew. And all the time that Wendy lived with us, we saw Nellie make her the most beautiful clothes we ever saw. But we never got anything pretty. Daddy asked Nellie to make Myrtle a dress for her graduation, and Nellie did just that.

She made her the simplest white dress she could make. There was absolutely nothing special about that dress. It was just a plain, straight up-and-down white dress. I could tell that Myrtle didn't like it at all, but she had no choice but to wear it. And so she did. When we all returned home from the graduation ceremony, Myrtle came straight in and took that dress off, put on her regular everyday dress, sat right in the big chair, opened a book, and started reading.

Everyone was quiet, not knowing what to make of her mood. But I knew. I knew she was upset that she had to wear that dress. Daddy made his way into the kitchen to start dinner. Nellie went to the bedroom as she usually did whenever Daddy started cooking. And the other kids went outside. I sat there on the sofa and watched as Myrtle sat there reading.

There was a stray cat that Nellie had claimed as her own and would sometimes let into the house to feed. While Myrtle was sitting in the chair reading, the cat jumped up on the arm of the chair and startled Myrtle. In a heated, mindless reaction, Myrtle grabbed that cat and threw it from the front of the house to the back.

"Get outa here, you dumb, stupid cat!"

I heard the cat let out a howl, and a loud thud followed.

Daddy yelled from the kitchen, "Hey! What's going on out there?"

Myrtle got up and ran out the front door down the street.

Nellie came out of the bedroom, looking around with those big bubble eyes. "Where's Myrtle? Did she do something to my cat?"

Then Nellie went into the kitchen and sat at the table to talk about Myrtle to my dad. "You're gonna have to do something about that girl. She done got to be too grown. I'd be willing to bet she went down there to Billy Washington's house. You know ever since, she been calling herself courting that boy, she has gotten to be too much to handle. She sasses me all the time. And she don't show me no kind of respect anymore. I know her and that Billy boy are having sex! I just know it!"

Daddy slammed something down on the table. "Whatchu mean? Are you saying this because you know something? Elizabeth, go down the street and get Myrtle right now!"

I got up and ran down the street to Billy Washington's house. I told Myrtle what Nellie told Daddy.

"What? Me and Billy ain't did a damn thing! I love him, but we ain't did nothing!"

"Well, Nellie is telling Daddy this whole big ole lie about you. And Daddy is really upset."

Billy Washington chimed in, "Wait a minute, wait a minute, let me go down there with you, Myrtle. I'm sure I can clear this whole thing up."

The three of us returned to the house, and as we approached the front steps, Myrtle turned to Billy and said, "Please, just wait out here on the porch. I'll go in and talk to him first, and if need be, I'll call you in to back me up."

So, Myrtle and I went into the house so she could talk to Daddy while Billy stayed back. By this time, Nellie had plopped herself down in the big chair as if she was waiting for a show to begin. Myrtle and I walked past her and headed straight for the kitchen where Daddy stood by the table.

He looked at me and said, "Elizabeth, you go somewhere and sit down." Then he looked at Myrtle and said, "You follow me."

They both went into the back bedroom and not more than a minute had gone by before I heard him yelling and the crack of his belt hitting Myrtle.

Whenever she got a whipping from Daddy, Myrtle refused to cry. Which would cause him to become even angrier, and he'd strike her even more, and she'd stand there and take it, but today was different. She didn't want to take it anymore.

Myrtle pushed past Daddy and ran out the door, past everybody and down to a friend's house to hide out. She even ran right past Billy who was still out front, pacing back and forth.

Daddy came out of the bedroom and looked around, looking for Myrtle. Then he came storming down the hallway to the front of the house and out the front door where he spotted Billy, pacing. He headed toward Billy, not saying a word, and started swinging. But Billy was too fast.

He was dodging every punch Daddy was throwing, all the while yelling, "Mr. Davidson, please! Listen to me. Whatever you think you know isn't true!"

After about a minute or two of Daddy trying to land a punch, he finally did. Billy, who was a tall, strapping young man, grabbed my daddy around the waist, picked him up, and slammed him down in the grass, falling on top of him. He quickly got up, stood back, and looked at my daddy lying there moaning, then Billy turned and ran all the way back toward his house to go look for Myrtle.

Two days passed before we finally got word from one of Myrtle's friends that Billy had given her $15 to leave town. She used $7 of it to buy a train ticket to Chicago, where she found a job within the week. I later found out that she was staying with a relative of our oldest brother, Walter, on his father's side of the family. When Walter moved out some years ago, he moved to Chicago and was living in the lower level of a two-family flat. His father's sister lived upstairs. So, she let Myrtle sleep on the couch until she was able to move out on her own.

When I heard the news, I was happy for Myrtle but sad too. I didn't want to be there in our home without her, but I still had my other siblings to worry about. One thing I knew for certain, Myrtle was happy to be away from Daddy's beatings and away from "that old black-ass Nellie," as Myrtle often called her.

It seemed to me that this was just the beginning of many big changes set to take place in my life. I felt like maybe I could've done something to prevent Daddy from whipping Myrtle and her leaving town. I'm not sure why I felt that it was my responsibility to try to help and protect everyone, but I guess it was my way of feeling needed. And ever since my mother died, that feeling grew and grew inside of me. It gave me some type of comfort to be needed. I certainly felt the void in my heart that came from my mother's passing, but the peculiar thing is, I didn't understand why I took it upon myself to try to be strong for everyone else when I, too, needed to feel supported and loved.

I was always a giving person. Not just of material things but of myself. I gave without regard or hidden expectations. I didn't worry about myself. I guess maybe it was because I felt that outside of my siblings, no one else really worried about me either. So, I chose to focus my attention on those less fortunate than me. This proved to be the case throughout the rest of my life. I learned early on the meaning of my name, and I intended on living up to it. Elizabeth in Hebrew means the oath of God. An oath is a solemn promise regarding a future action or behavior. I took pride in my name. I felt as if God himself had chosen that name for me, and with that, he had also given me an assignment. And I took my assignment seriously. If I ever made a promise, you better believe, come hell or high water, I was going to make it happen.

Now that it was a little over a year since Myrtle had left, I could see in my other siblings' behaviors that they, too, were wishing that they were old enough to make an exit plan. Carl Jr., however, was actually old enough to leave home. He had just turned eighteen and was talking about joining the military. And sure enough, not long after he shared this with me, he was on a bus headed for a training base somewhere. I think Gregory and Donald took it pretty hard when Carl Jr. left home.

Gregory, who was age sixteen at this point, started getting into trouble and doing things he knew we weren't raised to do. I got news from one of our neighborhood friends that they heard he was around town doing holdups for money. I didn't want to believe it, but I soon learned that it was true. One day, I was in the bedroom that he shared with Donald, and I was putting away in his chest of drawers some of his clothes that I had just washed. In the top drawer was a pistol covered over by a pair of socks. I was so upset that I ran outside to find him. When I confronted him about it, all he could do was stutter and try to explain himself. He always had a problem with stuttering, but it got worse when he was nervous.

"Na-na-na-na, Eh-Eh-Elizabeth, le-le-le-let me explain!"

"No, Gregory, I already know. I heard about the holdups you been doing. You already done had a run-in with the law. Do you want to go to jail? Or worse get killed?"

"Eh-Eh-Elizabeth, I just used it to ge-ge-get some m-m-m-m-m-money back from this guy who owed it to me. I sw-sw-swear I ain't gone do nothing else with it. I pr-pr-pr-promise!"

I don't know why I chose to believe him because not long after that, he was caught up in a situation that landed him in prison for murder, sentenced to life. And I felt somewhat responsible. I should've taken that gun from him. I should've said something to Daddy. I had the biggest feeling of regret, and it broke my heart, something terrible to see Gregory behind bars. He didn't mean to hurt or kill anyone. It was a very horrible mistake. He was actually a good person but was just caught up in a situation where he was defending himself and the other person was injured and died. But even with Gregory being in prison, he kept the faith that he wouldn't have to serve the full extent of his sentence.

At this point, I started to feel my foundation shake. Mama died when I was just a little girl; my oldest brother, Walter, got married and left home not long after that; then my sister, Myrtle, left home; then Carl Jr. left to join the Navy; then Gregory was sent to prison. At this point, it was just me, Doris, and Donald still there with Daddy and Nellie. And, of course, Judith, who still lived close by with her aunt.

I think that all these drastic changes had really started to affect Donald the most. I say this because he started showing signs of mental instability. One day, a lady in our neighborhood asked him to do some work for her. She wanted him to clear some brush from the field next to her home, plant some flowers, and dig up a small shrub on the side of her house. Donald went down there without a shovel or any tools and took care of everything. But just before his job was finished, he still needed to remove the shrub. With his bare hands, he took hold around the base of the shrub, and with a firm grip, he yanked it right up out the ground. When the lady saw him do this without any tools or any assistance, it must've scared her that he was so abnormally strong.

In a panicked manner, she asked him to leave without wanting to pay him for his labor. And since she refused to pay him, he got upset and verbally threatened her. She decided to call the police on him. When they arrived, it took four officers to restrain him and take him away. Thankfully, he was released soon after.

But about a month or so later, Donald had what folks call a mental breakdown and ended up strapped to one of those wheeled gurneys at the hospital. I can't believe how strong he was because, somehow, he managed to get up on his feet and actually tried to walk right out of that place while that thing was still strapped to him. Doris and I went down there and prayed with him and were able to convince him to stay and get the help he needed. Thankfully, he did get help and was able to officially leave a few weeks later.

After Donald returned home, things were back to normal for a little while. Daddy was still going to work every day, and Nellie had slowed down on her tyrannical behavior. Another year had come and gone, and I had just graduated from school. Judith, who was fifteen by this time, had also left her aunt's house in St. Louis, headed for Chicago. That summer was when I had decided that it was time for me to spread my wings too. After all, the only ones left at home were Doris, Donald, and me. Donald, who was sixteen, was making plans to go to Florida, and Doris had another two years of school left.

At age seventeen, I didn't want to make a permanent decision to leave, so I had the bright idea to try out life in Tennessee just for the summer. Thankfully, Daddy agreed to it. My mother had family there that owned farmland just south of Nashville in a county iron-ically called Davidson County, so I had it figured out in my mind that I'd be able to stay with them on the farm, find a job nearby, and save up enough money to be able to stand on my own for good. I was optimistic and ready for change. Nashville would surely be a new, fun, and exciting place to live, even if just for a little while. I grabbed the one other dress I owned, and a few other personal items, and headed south on the train.

CHAPTER THREE

# *You're All Grown Now*

My second cousin, Honey, and her husband, Henry, were proud owners of a beautiful piece of farmland in Tennessee, and they let me know that they were looking forward to my stay. That farm was the place where a lot of us migrated to during the summer months. Growing up, we had so much fun visiting and staying on that farm. So, I was certain that my time there that summer would not disappoint.

When I first arrived, I was greeted by a host of family members. Some of whom were there visiting for the week and were packing up to leave to go back to their individual homes. It was good to see folks I hadn't seen since my mother passed. But the person I was most excited to see was cousin Honey. I absolutely loved Honey.

"Little Elizabeth!" Honey yelled out as I exited the cab and approached the porch. "It's so wonderful to see you! Come on in here, chile, and take a load off. I know you're tired. Are you hungry? Did you eat? How was the train ride? I was so worried about you coming here all by yourself. Ooh-wee! I'm just so glad you're here!"

She carried on over me like it had been years since I was last there, but it was just two summers ago. Cousin Henry pulled at her arms that were gripping me tightly around my waist.

"Honey, let that gal go! My Lord, you'd think she was returning home from war!"

All I could do was fall out laughing. I liked the attention from Honey because she reminded me so much of my mother. She and my mother were first cousins, and they had very similar personalities. As a matter of fact, I was named after her. Her real name was Elizabeth. But we always referred to her as Honey because she was just so sweet.

Honey had a room all set up for me in the back of the house. I had my very own room with my very own bed. I was so pleased about that because all my life I had to share a foldaway bed with my sisters, and our bedroom was the living room of our home. So, to have this type of accommodation was exhilarating to say the least. Honey had even gone so far as to put a little personal note on my pillow, welcoming me. It made me feel so special. I hadn't felt that way in a very long time. I smiled as I read every word.

> Dear Elizabeth,
>
> It is such a blessing to have you here with us this summer. You be sure to help yourself to whatever you need while you're here. I want you to feel right at home. I hope you like your room, sweetheart. Please, let me know if you need anything at all.
>
> Love you much,
> Cousin Honey

I wiped away a lone tear that had escaped and made its way down my cheek. I hardly every cried. I guess I felt like crying made me feel too vulnerable. But the unconditional love I received from Honey was enough to make me feel safe and free to outwardly express whatever I was feeling on the inside.

After being there for a couple of days, I spent almost every waking moment right up under Honey, helping her do various chores around the house, preparing meals and such. I enjoyed that thoroughly. On my third or fourth evening there, Honey and I sat in the two rocking chairs on the front porch, laughing and talking about fond memories of my mother. We then moved to the subject of the purpose of my visit. Honey knew a member of her church that was the owner of a small restaurant, and she promised that she would inquire with him to see if he needed some help waiting tables. I was so excited and hopeful to be able to go to work right away.

Honey gave me the rundown. "While at church Sunday, I'll ask Brother Proctor if he needs any help at the restaurant. I know he had his son down there helping to run the place, but he just recently left to join the military, so he ain't got nobody to help take up the slack yet. So, timing couldn't be better. I can take you to the main road every morning, and there's a bus stop right there that can take you right into the part of town where the restaurant is. How does that sound?"

"Oh, that's just fine with me, Honey. I truly appreciate you for this. What can I do to pay my keep while I'm here?"

"Baby, you just go to work, save your money, and just be sure to save up so you can make whatever goal you done set for yourself. All I ask is that you help me around here like you been doing for the past few days, ya hear?"

"Yes, ma'am. Thank you so much."

When Sunday rolled around, we were all standing around after service, and I was introduced to Brother Proctor. He was a very light-complexioned and handsome man with gray eyes. He looked to be maybe in his fifties. And on his arm was a very beautiful woman who happened to be his wife. I can remember standing there admiring how well put together they both looked and how loving they seemed to be toward each other as she stood by his side, smiling, with her arm intertwined with his. Brother Proctor and Honey had just discussed me working for him, and it was all set. I was to start work there the next day.

Monday morning had come, and I was up early, sitting at the kitchen table waiting on Honey to drop me off at the bus stop. I wanted to be to work on time, and I wanted to be sure that Brother Proctor's first impression of me would be a good one. Once I got dropped off, I waited for the bus, and it came within the first five minutes of me standing there. I was able to sit back and enjoy the ride across town.

The bus drop-off point was about a half mile from the restaurant, so I had to walk the rest of the way. I arrived at Proctor's restaurant a few minutes before it was time to open. And about a minute or so after I had arrived, Brother Proctor pulled up in front of the place in a beautiful 1946 emerald green Cadillac. My mouth near 'bout hit the ground. I had never in my life seen a black man own this type of automobile. I simply could not believe it. He was a wealthy and well-known businessman in town.

"Well, Elizabeth, what do you say, let's get this day started, huh?"

I smiled sheepishly. "Yes, sir. What would you like for me to do first?"

"Once we get going, you can help by keeping the main dining area nice and clean by wiping down tables and sweeping up after folks are done eating. I'll also need you to do a little work in the back by keeping track of supplies and such. How does that sound?"

"Sounds good to me. Whatever you need done. I'm here to work hard, and hopefully you'll be satisfied with my performance."

He looked me directly in my eyes. "Oh, I'm certain I will."

As the customers started pouring in, I made sure to greet each one as they entered the restaurant and offered them a cool drink of water. I wanted to be sure to give the best service while I worked in the restaurant. I was hoping that maybe Brother Proctor would take notice of me enough to keep me on for longer than just the summer.

There was a total of five employees in the restaurant, including Brother Proctor. It appeared that he only personally served the more distinguished customers (businessmen, educators, preachers, and such) while the other workers served the more "common folk." I was impressed with the steady stream of customers coming through the door. That restaurant stayed busy, which made my workday fly by.

However, there was one customer that caught my attention. It was a beautiful young woman who came in and sat in the section where Brother Proctor worked. She sat there quietly, sipping on a hot cup of coffee until she made eye contact with Brother Proctor, and they both headed to the back of the restaurant. They weren't back there very long, but I just wondered who she was and why they were back there.

When they emerged from the back, they both were smiling, and she was giggling so hard that I rolled my eyes at how she was carrying on. I mean Brother Proctor was a very attractive man and all, but after all he was married, and it all just didn't seem right to me. But I was determined to mind my business and stay focused on what I was there to do.

Later in the day, near closing time, there were just a few customers left and just about time for me to end my workday. I was sweeping up wasted food from around the tables and chairs when Brother Proctor walked over to me and placed his hand on my shoulder.

"Okay, Elizabeth, that about does it for the day, my dear. Do you need a ride home?"

"Oh no, sir, I rode the bus here, and I'll be going back the same way."

"Well, you be safe out there. I wouldn't want anything to happen to you." Then he winked and said, "Your cousin Honey and I go way back, and I promised her that I would take good care of you."

"Thank you, Brother Proctor. I sure appreciate it, but I'll be fine."

After my shift, I made my half-mile walk back and waited for my bus, smiling all the way. I felt so accomplished and satisfied with how my first day turned out. I couldn't wait to tell Honey all about it. Once I made it to my final destination, Honey was right there waiting on me. She was smiling from ear to ear, and so was I.

I hopped up in her pickup truck, and we zoomed down the dirt road toward the farm. I told her all about my day, and she was so happy and relieved that everything went well. I saved back the little tidbit about that lady coming in and going to the back of the restaurant with Brother Proctor. I didn't want to come across a busybody and speak on something I had no business speaking on. So, I kept my mouth shut regarding that. Besides, after I had given it more thought, she could've just been a relative of his, for all I knew.

Honey interrupted my thoughts. "Well, I'm sure glad you had a successful day today, sugar. You just keep on doing what you're doing, and soon enough, you'll be sitting on a pile of money! Hahaha! Now go get washed up for supper. I have a nice meal prepared to celebrate your first day at your job."

"Whew! Yes, ma'am!" I replied with such enthusiasm that we both fell out laughing.

Everybody knows I love me some good cooking. And Honey was one of the best cooks I knew, second to Daddy, of course.

Days turned into weeks, and I had my daily routine running like clockwork. Things were going according to plan. I finally had a feeling of accomplishment, along with love and support from Honey. After working at the restaurant for about a month, I figured that after work, I'd go to a nearby dress shop and purchase myself a brand-new dress. I had been wearing the same two dresses for the past two years, so it was definitely time to buy a new one.

After work, I walked three blocks down to the dress shop. I knew that I only had a few minutes to spare because I didn't want to miss my bus. I moved as quickly as I could through the store on my search for a comfortable yet relatively nice-looking dress. I settled on a decent light blue cotton dress, paid the cashier, and scurried out the door.

Out of breath and in a slight panic, I was moving twice as fast as usual in hopes that I had not missed my bus. But after standing at the bus stop for a while, I realized that I had. So, I started walking toward the next stop going in the direction toward home, thinking that this might help shave off some time lost from missing the previous bus. It was my hope that another one would be along soon, and I could just jump on that one.

But another one didn't come along, and I was starting to get nervous, and it was getting late. I didn't want Honey to start worrying. After I'd walked about two miles, a taxi cab pulled up to the curb while I was walking.

"Hey, young lady. You need a ride?"

I waved him off. "No, thank you. I missed my bus, but I'm going to catch the next one."

"Well, I'm just gonna tell you it's not too safe for a young girl like yourself to be walking out here alone, especially since it's getting close to the evening hours. There's always folks just looking to bring harm to a young lady such as yourself, ya know?"

Exhausted and slightly irritated, I said, "Well, I appreciate your concern, sir, but I don't have the money to pay for a taxi."

"Oh, you say you don't? Well, where you live? If it's not too far, I'll be a Good Samaritan and get you there, no problem."

I was a little hesitant but thought about how late it already was and how it was taking so long for the next bus to come and how tired my feet were and how worried Honey would be if I didn't make it to our meeting location soon. The way I figured it, at this rate, it might be after dark before I made it there.

"I live about nine miles that way." I pointed in the direction I was headed. "You can just drop me off at the bus stop at the corner of Sycamore Road. I have a relative who's there waiting to take me the rest of the way home."

"Oh, okay. Well, hop on in, and I'll get you where you need to be, and don't worry about the cost. The pleasure is all mine."

So, I tossed my new dress over my arm, opened the rear door of the taxi, and got in. As he pulled away from the curb, he asked me if I lived around that location long because he knew pretty much everyone in town and didn't remember seeing me. I told him I was in town for the summer from St. Louis, visiting family.

He replied with a little excitement in his voice. "Oh, yeah? I've got family in St. Louis too! So, you're just out doing some shopping, huh?"

"No, sir, I work at Proctor's restaurant a couple of miles back the other way. And after work, I stopped to buy myself a new dress."

"Oh, okay. Yeah, I know of Mr. Proctor. He seems like a nice guy. He does a lot in the community."

We continued to make small talk as we drove along. We were a few miles up the road when he prematurely turned down the wrong street.

"Excuse me, sir. You're going the wrong way. You should've kept straight about another mile or so."

"I know. I forgot I have to get some gasoline, and I have a service station I like to go to, and it's this way. Don't worry. It'll only take me a few minutes to fill this old girl up, and we'll be back on course. I'll have you to your folks in no time."

We drove about another mile to a narrow back road and turned into a large dirt lot that was right next to some sort of old vacant building.

As we drove into the lot, he said, "Oh, hell! Did you feel that? I think my back tire done went flat."

"No, I didn't feel anything."

"Yeah, I think it's definitely my tire. I need to get out and take a look at it."

He put the taxi in park, opened his door, and stepped out. He came around to my side of the vehicle and was looking down at the tire with his hand on my door. Then, all of a sudden, my door swung open, and he was standing right at my side. He pushed me over in the seat with such force that it disoriented me. Then he got into the back seat next to me and started holding me down while he undid his pants.

I screamed, "What the hell are you doing?"

"Shut the hell up!"

He backslapped me across my face. I tasted blood from my nose as it poured down into my mouth, and I let out a loud howl. He then pulled up my dress and ripped off my panties. I clawed and kicked as much as I could when out of nowhere, *wham!* He hit me again.

At that moment, I felt that if I continued to fight him, he'd become even more aggressive. So, I resorted to crying and begging him to stop. But it was like he didn't even hear me. He kept going until he was able to get his pants down far enough to release himself and penetrate me. It hurt so bad! It felt like I was on fire. The pressure from him thrusting himself into me caused me to let out yet another howl. I was screaming in pain, but nothing seemed to distract him from continuing to violate me.

I felt his stinking breath on my neck, escaping in hot, forced bursts of air with each thrust he delivered. And each time he thrust himself into me, I felt closer and closer to death. By this point, I thought that he would surely kill me once he was done. He suddenly let out a loud yell, followed by several grunts, and he fell limp on top of me. He lay there for what seem like an eternity, breathing heavy and moaning. I waited quietly to see what he would do next. He put his hand over my mouth and looked me dead in my eyes.

"If you tell anybody about this, I'll kill you. You hear me? I swear to you, I'll do it. I know where you work, so I know how to find you. You understand me?"

He lifted his hand from my mouth and allowed me to answer through my tears.

"Yes…"

He slid off me and stood up by my door and pulled his pants back up to fasten them. Then he reached into his pocket, pulled out a handkerchief, and handed it to me. "Good. Take this. Wipe your face and stop crying. Shit, I know damn well that a big, full-bodied girl like yourself done been with a man before, and I know you liked it. Now stop all that crying and get yourself together."

He tightened up his belt and slammed the door. Then he walked back around to the driver's door, got in, started the engine, and pulled off with the tires kicking up dirt, leaving a cloud of dust behind as if it was marking the spot where I lost my innocence. He drove back to the main road and headed in the direction of my drop-off spot. But he stopped and let me out less than a mile away.

"You remember what I said, gal. You bet not tell a soul. You hear?"

Through my whimpers, I responded, "Yes."

"Good. Now get out!"

I opened the rear door, stepped out of the taxi, and turned around to grab my new dress that was crumpled on the floor. I stood back and grabbed the door handle to close it. He pulled away so fast that I barely had a chance to move my hand once the door was closed.

I was in shock and in so much pain. I couldn't believe what had just happened to me. As I walked up the road to meet Honey, I caught a glimpse of myself in a storefront window. I stepped toward the glass to get a closer look at my face. My hair was disheveled, blood was smeared across my face, and I had a bruise on my left cheek. There was no cleaning up and hiding this before anyone saw me.

I heard Honey blowing the horn and yelling from her pickup truck a few feet away. "Elizabeth! Elizabeth! Where have you been? Come on, sugar. I have a roast in the oven, and I don't want it to burn!"

As I approached her, my heart tried to beat out of my chest. I didn't want her to know what just happened, but there was no way to avoid it.

"My Lord, chile. What in the world happened to you?"

I couldn't give a response to her question. I just kept my head down and mumbled, "Please, Honey, let's just go. Please."

We drove just a little way on our way back to the farm when she suddenly pulled over.

"Listen, I understand you don't want to tell me, but I can't help you unless you do. Elizabeth, who did this to you? Was it someone on the bus?"

I shook my head no.

"Okay…uhhh…did it happen at the store where you got that dress?"

Again, I shook my head no. She questioned me for the next couple of minutes until I just broke down sobbing. I tried my best to tell her what happened, but all I could muster up was a jumbled explanation.

"I missed the bus. I didn't want you to worry. Then the taxi came. He turned too soon. I told him he made a wrong turn…but-but he said he needed gas. Then he stopped and got out. Then… then he…"

"Then he what, baby?" she asked in stock-still anticipation of what I was about to say next.

"He-he…hit me and-and…" I couldn't finish. But she knew what happened next.

"Elizabeth, did he force himself on you?"

Though sobbing and shaking uncontrollably, I managed to nod my head yes. She reached over and hugged me tight while we sat there in that old pickup truck. She didn't care about the roast still cooking in the oven. She hugged me until I stopped crying. She let the roast burn that night.

Thankfully, it was Friday, and I didn't have to go to work the next day. I slept in a little the next morning and was awakened by the loud roaring of cousin Henry's tractor. My bedroom window was slightly cracked, and the comforting aroma of cut grass flowed in. I lay there for a while in somewhat of a daze when I heard a light knock at my door. It was Honey coming to check on me.

"Elizabeth, may I come in?"

"Yes."

She slowly opened the door, came in, and sat on the edge of my bed. She put her hand on my cheek and looked at me like I was an ailing child.

"How you feeling, sweetheart? You need me to get you anything?"

"No, I'm okay. Thank you. What time is it?"

"It's almost noon."

My body was still sore from the trauma of the day before, so it took some effort to shift my position enough to sit up in the bed.

"Ohhh... I don't think I've ever slept in this late. I'm so sorry. I just..."

She interrupted. "No, sugar. There's no need for any apologies. You need the rest. Listen, Elizabeth...I would understand if you didn't want to go back to work at the restaurant. We can find you somewhere else to work. That's only if you feel up to it."

"Honey, thank you. But I don't want to stop working there. I'll be okay. I need the money, and I like it there."

"Well, when that bus lets you off in the morning, you need to hightail it straight to that restaurant, you hear me? And I'm going to ask Brother Proctor to take you to the bus stop after you get off work and wait with you until your bus arrives."

"Thank you, Honey, but I don't..."

"Elizabeth, I have to take a stand on this. I'm not allowing you to return there otherwise. I'll be damned if I allow you to be back in a situation where that bastard can hurt you again!"

43

"Yes, ma'am. Okay." I had to agree with her. Maybe that was best.

Monday rolled around, and Honey let me use some of her pancake foundation makeup to cover my bruise. She then took me to my drop-off point, and I got right on the bus. Once I made it to my stop, I did just as she instructed. When that bus let me off a half mile from the restaurant, I double-timed it all the way there.

When I arrived at the restaurant, I was sweating and panting so hard that Brother Proctor took notice. Honey had told him, while they were at church the day before, that she wanted him to wait with me at the bus stop after work, but I certainly hope she didn't tell him the reason behind it.

"Good morning, Elizabeth. You training for the Olympic games or something? Why are you so out of breath?"

"Oh, I…umm…I, uh…I just…"

"I'm just kidding with you. Come on to the back. I have some dishcloths that need to be folded and put away. You can sit at the table back there and rest your feet for a bit while you fold them. You'll have an easy day today. Monday's are usually slow around here anyways. You need anything? Would you like a cup of coffee?"

"No, thank you."

In the back of my mind, I wondered if Honey actually did tell him what happened to me, and this made me a bit apprehensive. If he did indeed know then, his use of humor about me training for the Olympic games was inappropriate. If he didn't know then, why was he being so accommodating? I took a seat at the table and got straight to work folding the dishcloths. After a few minutes, Brother Proctor came and sat across from me at the table.

"Listen, your cousin Honey told me that she wants me to take you to the bus stop each day for the rest of your time working here this summer and wait with you. You wanna tell me what happened between Friday and today that has her so protective of you all of a sudden?"

I let out a big sigh of relief that Honey hadn't said anything, but I was also a bit irritated that he wanted an explanation from me.

"Um, well, somebody tried to bother me, so she thought it best to ask you to wait with me until the bus comes. But I understand if you're not able to do it. I can just..."

"No, no, no problem. I was just curious. Don't worry, darling. It's fine."

"Thank you."

Just then the little bell that hung on the front door of the restaurant jingled to let him know he had his first customer of the day. He got up from the table to go see who it was. I could hear him whispering to someone, so I lightly tiptoed to the door to get in better earshot and to hopefully sneak a peek at who he was talking with so secretively.

Lo and behold, it was that same lady from a few weeks back. She was standing pressed up against Brother Proctor like she was about to give him a good old-fashioned rubdown. I saw him put his arms around her waist and give her one of the sloppiest kisses I'd ever had the displeasure of beholding. I couldn't believe it. He was cheating on his wife!

I quickly turned around to go back to folding when my foot inadvertently kicked over the broom propped up next to the doorframe. They were both startled by the noise and swung their heads in my direction, looking like a couple of deer caught in car headlights. I rushed back to the table, regretting that I'd even made the attempt to see who it was.

A few minutes later, the bell jingled again. Then the sound of his footsteps echoed in my ears as they drew closer and louder. My heart was racing with the anticipation of Brother Proctor confronting me on what I had just witnessed. He approached the table and chuckled slightly as he took his seat. We sat there in silence for a few seconds. I kept folding the cloths, not wanting to give any eye contact, when he suddenly reached across the table and touched my hands, halting their feverish movements. I dared not look up at him, so I just sat there and stared down at my chest as I watched it rise and fall at a rapid pace.

"Elizabeth..." He waited a few seconds, and when I didn't answer, he called my name again.

"Yes, sir?"

"I know that you saw me and my lady friend, Miss Harriet, up front there, right?"

"Yes, sir."

With a big sigh and the sound of disappointment in his voice, he continued. "Huh…well, I guess we both have something we need to keep secret then, don't we?"

With that, I jerked my head up with intense curiosity about what he meant by that. "Pardon?"

"Oh, I think you know what I'm talking about. You keep my secret, and I'll keep yours."

I lowered my head again, totally lost for words. I couldn't believe that Honey actually told him what happened to me. I was so embarrassed and ashamed. He got up from his chair, stepped closer to me, and bent down in such a way as to get a better look at my face.

"Yeah, you know exactly what I'm talking about, don't you? You only have three more weeks here, so I'd advise you to keep your mouth shut, and there won't be any issues for me or you."

I didn't respond. But I knew that the next few weeks were going to be extremely uncomfortable for me, so I began to calculate a reason to quit so that Honey wouldn't know that I knew what she told him. And I definitely didn't want her to know about his lady friend, Miss Harriet. I resolved it in my mind. That week would be my last week there.

I went through the remainder of the week, working for Brother Proctor in almost complete silence, only responding to him when necessary. And as for the time he waited with me at the bus stop until my bus came, I stood outside his car at the stop. When my bus came, I politely waved him off and went on my way.

By Thursday evening, I had settled on a lie to tell Honey. I would tell her that I was offered another job to do some light housework for a customer who came into the restaurant. I'd tell her that the woman's maid fell ill and she needed someone to fill in for just a couple of weeks. By then it would be time for me to head back home to St. Louis. It wasn't a perfect plan, but it was the best one I had at the time. My only concern was that I hadn't really saved as much money as I would've liked. But I had to make it work until I could return home.

Friday morning arrived, and as usual, things were tense between me and Brother Proctor. However, since Fridays were one of the busiest days at the restaurant, we didn't have to interact much. As the day rolled toward closing time, I started to feel some relief. I'd let him know that this would be my last day, I would collect my earnings, and we wouldn't have to ever see each other again. He could keep his dirty little secret, and I could get on with my life.

It was the end of the day, and the last patron was leaving. I was in the back tidying up and could hear Brother Proctor wrapping things up. A few minutes later, he came to the back and asked me if I was ready to go.

"Um, yes. But I need to tell you that today is my last day. Would it be possible to collect my earnings for the week?"

He sounded surprised. "What chu mean today is your last day? You've got a couple more weeks to work here for me. You ain't trying to skirt around that understanding we got between us, are you?"

My voice shook with nervousness. "No, no, it's just I was offered a housekeeping job that pays a little bit more, and I need more money in order to meet my goal before going back to St. Louis."

"Oh, you need more money, huh? How bad do you need it?"

He took hold of the collar of my dress and pulled me in close to him. Then he put one hand around my waist and used his other hand to grab my breasts. He began tugging at the buttons on the front of my dress. I pulled away so quickly that he ripped off one of the buttons. He laughed and grabbed me again even tighter while forcibly kissing me.

He pushed me down on a dusty old loveseat near the back door, where the workers would go to take a smoke break. He started unfastening his pants. I lay there for a few seconds in shock and shivering, reliving in my mind what had happened to me at the hands of that cab driver. But the anger I felt from being violated all over again rose up in me so fierce that I had to do something drastic and quick. While he was kissing me on my neck, I opened my mouth wide and chomped down on his earlobe until I drew blood. He hollered and let go of me to grab hold of his ear.

"Get the hell out of my restaurant! I ain't giving you a damn dime!

I leaped up, pushed past him, and ran out the front door. I kept running all the way down the street toward the bus stop. I was a few yards away from the stop and could see that the bus was already there and about to pull off. I picked up speed and yelled as loud as I could to catch the driver's attention. Thankfully, he heard me. I paid my fair and sat down crying uncontrollably.

No one on that bus even bothered to ask me if I was okay. They just rode along in silence, making an obvious effort to ignore my sobs. By the time I reached my drop-off point, I had composed myself enough to have the courage to tell Honey what just happened. I was certain that she and cousin Henry would handle him. I knew that they would expose his perverted ass to his wife and the church and maybe even be able to make him pay the money he owed me.

I exited the bus and saw Honey's pickup truck idling just a few feet away from the bus stop. I approached and got in slowly. Honey reached down and grabbed the hem of her housedress, dabbed the beads of perspiration on her forehead with it, and looked over at me.

"Whew! Lord! It's hotter than blue blazes out here today! I had a long day full of chores, and I ain't had no time to start supper before coming to get you. So, hopefully, you can help me with the cooking tonight. I swear sometimes I wish I could just run away to New York somewhere and live life in the big city. Hahaha! How was your day, honey?"

I was thinking of a proper way to explain my day. It must've taken me too long because she took a quick glance over at me to see what had my attention other than her complaining.

"What's the matter with you, chile? The cat got your tongue or something?"

I figured that I might as well just get it over with and not beat around the bush. Besides, at this point, I was so mad. Mad at the whole situation. And quite honestly, I was upset with Honey for even saying anything to that bastard about what happened to me in the first place. I couldn't help but think that if he never knew then, maybe he wouldn't have thought that he could hold it over my head and be so bold as to violate me as well. So, yeah, I was pretty upset and felt like exploding.

"Your friend, Brother Proctor, is a lowlife bastard! And he ain't what everybody thinks he is. He tried to hurt me, Honey! He tried to hurt me because he knew about the other man that hurt me. He kept my money too, and I don't know what I'm going to do!"

"Wait, what are you talking about, Elizabeth?"

"I know you told him what happened to me! Why would you do that? Why would you tell him that! He took that and used it against me to keep me from telling anyone that I saw him kissing that woman. He knew I saw them, so he threatened to embarrass me about what happened to me if I told!"

"Elizabeth, are you sure about all this? You sure you ain't got things mixed up?"

I was upset with her suggestion that I was confused. "What do you mean 'mixed up,' Honey? I know what the man said to me! And I definitely know what he tried to do to me!"

"Wait, Elizabeth, now what you're saying about this man is really bad, so I want you to be sure that whatever you say really did happen. I mean, after all, he's a good friend to our family, he's on the deacon board at the church, and he has high standing in the community. He does a lot of good for the local college kids, the elderly, and everybody. Now I know he's a good-looking man and a lot of the young girls in town swoon all over him. But I ain't never heard no stories about him cheating on his wife with no woman, let alone messing around with no young gals!"

"Honey, I know you're not saying that you think I tried something with him, are you? Or worse, that I'm lying about what he tried to do to me?"

"Elizabeth, I'm just trying to make this make sense to me. I mean behind what happened to you, it ain't been but a week, you know. So, I can't help but think that maybe you still swirling from all of that. I mean maybe you think all of this happened in your mind, but..."

"Wait a minute, Honey. Just wait one minute! I may be a lot of things but a liar, I am not! And I for damn sure ain't crazy! Now if you think that I would sit up here and make up all of this or if you expect me to accept the notion that my mind is just playing tricks on me, then take a look at my dress! See this ripped hole where the button used to be? And do you see this bloodstain right here? Yeah… he tried to unbutton my dress, and I snatched away from him and he ripped it. And the blood is from where I bit a plug in that bastard's ear! So, don't tell me I'm lying or that I'm crazy. I know what in the hell happened to me! I wish I never even came down here. I should've stayed in St. Louis, and none of this would've ever happened to me! But you know what? Had you had the decency to keep what happened to me to yourself, maybe he wouldn't have even thought to do what he did to me. Now I gotta deal with this on top of what I went through last week!"

"What are you saying to me, chile? Are you saying all of this is my fault?"

I didn't answer her. But my nonresponse said it all. I think she knew that in that moment, my feelings of adoration I had for her were tarnished for good. In that moment, I lost the only person that I felt cared for me like a mother, and the only feelings and emotions left were tremendous pain and disappointment.

"Well, tell you what… if you believe that, then you can just take yourself right on back to St. Louis. I don't need this! I ain't been nothing but good to you, and now you wanna blame me for *your* issues. You're all grown now and think you know everything, huh? I can't believe this!"

"You want to know what I can't believe, Honey? I can't believe you feel it's more important to protect the reputation of that man than it is to believe your own flesh and blood. But don't worry, I'll leave and go back home first thing tomorrow."

The next morning, before the sun rose, I packed up my stuff and left. I walked all the way to the main road, caught the bus to the train station, and bought a one-way ticket back home to St. Louis.

CHAPTER FOUR

# *My Dear, Sweet Love*

Returning home from Tennessee before the summer was over was not something I had anticipated. But the way my life was going, I probably shouldn't have tried to anticipate anything going the way I planned it. Once I got back home, things weren't much better.

By this time, my youngest brother, Donald, had left home also. The house wasn't the same neat and tidy place filled with laughter and fun. Daddy wasn't doing well physically, so he wasn't able to work as much. So, I offered up the money I had saved to help lighten his load a little. The cupboards were pretty bare, and Nellie was of no use at all. It had gotten so bad that I found myself going some days without eating.

I remember walking home from looking for a job and passing by a restaurant that had such a wonderful aroma coming from it. I didn't have any money, and there certainly wasn't anything to eat at home. So, I went behind the restaurant and found a pan of beans that were burnt on the bottom in the garbage. I was so hungry that I stuck my hand down in the pot and scooped out a handful of beans and ate until I got down to the burned part. After my belly was somewhat satisfied, the realization of what I had resorted to made me go into an emotional shutdown. I was sad and defeated. I needed some ray of hope and light to lead me up out of the state of despair I was in.

I had been back in St. Louis for about a month and was attending church regularly again in an attempt to find some direction and peace of mind. There was a lady at church named Mother Walton. She was a beautiful spirit. She took a liking to me and eventually

51

invited me to live with her. She had a nice two-story home where she allowed me to stay in one of the bedrooms upstairs. My time living with Mother Walton allowed me to learn and grow in my walk with God and to grow as a young woman.

I had just turned eighteen about a month prior. Although I was officially an adult, I still needed a positive female influence in my life. She taught me so much about the Bible and about life in general. She was an Evangelist, and she truly loved the Lord. I specifically remember one thing she shared with me about how in the Old Testament people did what was called a burnt offering. It was a sacrifice done as a tribute to God. There were a few reasons why a burnt offering would be given—atonement for sin was the main reason. I decided that I wanted to do something that would show God how much I loved and trusted him. The past few years of my life were very difficult and especially the past few months, so I needed a miraculous change.

One night after Mother Walton and I got home from church, I decided to go upstairs and prepare my own version of a burnt offering to the Lord. I took a sheet of paper and tore it into small pieces, then I wrote specific things down on each piece, my promises to him and a few things I wanted from him. I took those small pieces of paper and put them in a porcelain bowl, struck a match, and burned them. I promised God that if he would bless me to be healthy and financially stable, I would always be a blessing to others and never turn a soul away that needed help. This was part of my covenant with him.

I attended church faithfully, regardless of what I bore witness to among the so-called sanctified folks who were also attending the church. There was so much dirty business going on that if I kept my focus on the people, I would have walked away for sure. But I was determined to maintain my focus on my own personal relationship with God and not let anyone distract me from it.

I must say that I did encounter one interesting person who was at the church. She was new in town, and she had a lot of spunk. I liked that about her. Her name was Marla, and she was my age, just a few months older than me. She and I clicked instantly. We became best friends almost overnight. I mean, we literally started doing everything together, and we eventually even got jobs together at a tent-making factory.

Marla and I hung together like wet clothes. So much so that some of the busybodies down at the church started running their mouths about our friendship. This one deacon in particular started a rumor accusing us of being lovers. And anyone who may have grown up in a super religious church knows that if a rumor like that gets around, you are bound to be shamed and perhaps even put out of the church.

When I found out about deacon busybody telling folks that he saw me and Marla leaving a motel room together on the sketchy side of town at six o'clock in the morning, I was furious. I couldn't believe that someone would take out the time to make up such an outright lie.

This was the same deacon who told me that I ought not to wear open-toed shoes and short sleeve tops at church.

"Now, Sister Elizabeth, you know that here at Kennedy Temple Church of God in Christ, we don't want the women to wear shoes that show your toes or tops that show your arms. You have to remember, you are here to serve and worship the Lord, not to put on a show."

"Deacon, I'm not sure I understand what the issue is with what I have on."

"Well, because it might cause some of the men who might be struggling in a certain area to have unclean thoughts, if you know what I'm saying."

"With all due respect, Deacon, if my toes and elbows cause a man to fall into sin, then I have to wonder if he was ever truly saved in the first place!"

Needless to say, he didn't appreciate my response, but that shut him up right away and left him with nothing else to say. But he obviously felt like he needed to get back at me because I could see no other reason why he would spread such an outrageous rumor about me and Marla. Marla was my best friend, nothing more. I wasn't going to stand by and let him think that he could get away with flat-out lying about us.

On a following Sunday, he was up near the front of the church talking with some of the members. I walked right through the gathered cluster of folks and straight up to him.

"Excuse me, Deacon, may I please speak with you in private?"

He looked at me like I was leper. "Well, I am a little busy at moment. What is it?"

I took a big breath. "I really would like to be able to say what I need to say to you in private, please."

"Sister Elizabeth, you can say whatever it is you need to say to me right here. The deacon board and usher board are getting ready to hold a joint meeting right here, and I'm not about to step away to have some private conversation with you."

I gave a "it's-on-you" shrug of my shoulders.

"Okay then. Well…there's this rumor circulating that Marla and I are lovers and that you saw us coming out of a motel on the sketchy side of town at six o'clock in the morning. First, let me say that this is totally not true. But what I would like to know is if you really want to stand by the claim you've made, then I think what many of the members here would most be interested in knowing is what *you* were doing there at a motel on that side of town at six o'clock in the morning. And I'm most certain it wasn't evangelizing!"

From the expression on his face, I could tell that he was shocked that I would even have the nerve to confront him. But I didn't care. Wrong is wrong, and I couldn't care less about him being my elder, a man, or a deacon for that matter. I just wanted him to get a clear understanding that I was by no means intimidated by him or his standing in the church.

I didn't allow him an opportunity to respond. I promptly turned on the heels of my open-toed shoes and walked straight down the middle aisle and out through the double doors. I just left him there, with all the other deacon and usher board members, with their mouths hanging open. It felt so good to tell him off in front of all of them. I was sick of everybody looking at me like I was some tramp.

I wasn't going to allow anyone else to get away with making me feel less than. I'd had enough of that for the past ten years.

As the weeks and months passed and I grew into my woman-hood a bit more, I started to become more and more emboldened. I was starting to learn myself and embrace the part of me that was fearless. I didn't like the title of victim or the role one would have to play to wear that title. I wasn't just a survivor either. I was a conqueror!

Another year had come, and I was about nineteen years old and working hard at the tent-making factory. I had even earned enough money to purchase myself a half-decent used car. One afternoon, Marla and I were supposed to meet up at a local ice cream parlor after I got off work. But Marla had started dating this guy named Woody. He had her head in the clouds so much that she cancelled on me at the last minute. I decided that I was going to go to the parlor on my own, have a tall chocolate milkshake, and go home.

When I got there, it was just before the afternoon rush of folks with their kids started to pour in. I was sitting alone at the counter when a very handsome gentleman came up and stood right next to me and asked the soda jerk to make him an ice cream float. My pulse started to race a bit. He was so handsome that it made me nervous. I had never felt this nervous before. The smell of his cologne made me want to close my eyes and take in a deep breath to inhale his essence, but I managed to restrain my impulse to do so.

I held my head as if I were looking straight ahead but strained my eyes to the side in his direction to see if he was wearing a wedding band. When I saw that there was no ring, or a tan line where a ring might've been, I smiled on the inside.

He looked to be in his late twenties or early thirties. He was tall and had a dark complexion, with big, beautiful amber-colored eyes and wavy hair. He was one good-looking cat! He was sporting a tailored suit and wing-tipped shoes. He caught me checking him out and smiled then chuckled. I was nearly blinded by his gleaming white smile. I was smitten, and I think he knew it.

"Hello, my name is Arnold. And yours?"

I kept my answers short because I was so nervous. "Elizabeth."

"Pleasure to meet you, Elizabeth. Do you live or work in the area?"

"Both."

"Oh, really? Well this must be your first time in here because I stop through once or twice a week, and I've never seen you in here before.

"Um-hmm."

He took a seat on the stool right next to me and turned toward me. "Where do you work, if you don't mind me asking?"

I didn't give him any eye contact. I was too nervous. I just kept looking down at my milkshake.

"At Steinburg Tent Company. We make tents for the military."

"Oh, really? I have a cousin who works there. He seems to like it. How about you?"

"It's okay. It pays the bills."

"Yeah, I hear you."

There was a long pause and an awkward silence while he waited for his float. I tapped my nails on the countertop with one hand while stirring my drink with the other.

"Not much for conversation, huh?"

Knowing that I heard and understood what he said, I acted as if I didn't hear him. "Pardon?"

"I said, you're not much for conversation, are you?"

"Oh, I'm sorry. I guess I'm a little preoccupied with my thoughts."

"Really now? Would you like to share?"

I shifted myself on the stool and resolved that I might as well muster up the nerve to properly engage him in conversation. "Well, I was just sitting here thinking about a friend I was supposed to meet here after work, but they changed their plans on me at the last minute."

He leaned back in an exaggerated fashion as if he was shocked. "What! You mean to tell me that some cat let down a beautiful woman like yourself and left you to sit here all alone?"

"Oh, no. I'm not speaking of a man. I was actually referring to a female friend of mine."

"So…you're not attached to anyone?"

My heart started to race, and I fought back a smile that was trying its best to take over my lips.

"No, not at the present time."

"Wait! Is that a smile? My goodness, I got a smile. And it's a pretty smile at that!"

We both laughed and sat there a while talking and smiling at each other. The ice was broken, and I felt a little more at ease talking to him. I must say, he had me feeling like we'd known each other for years. We had such a good time that we agreed to meet there again the following week.

The next week came, and I made sure to wear one of my best dresses to work and tried all day not to mess it up. I wanted to be nice and presentable when I met Arnold again. When I arrived at the ice cream parlor, he was sitting at a table near the back waiting for me. When he saw me, he waved me over to him. When I approached the table, he stood up and pulled out my chair.

"I was determined to make it here before you. I didn't want you to think that I wasn't going to show."

"Well, I appreciate that, Arnold."

"I ordered you the same thing you had last time. I hope that was okay. And I think I'll try out the milkshake too. I usually get the same thing every time. But today I think something different would be nice."

I smiled in agreement, placed my pocketbook on the table, locked my fingers together, and leaned in toward him.

"So…the last time we were here, I never asked you what you did for a living."

"I'm a mortician. I work at A.W. Byrd Funeral Home on Lucas Avenue."

"Really? How do you like doing that?"

He looked at me with a slight smirk on his face. "It's okay. It pays the bills."

We both laughed because I knew he was mocking me for the answer I had given him the week prior.

"The truth is, I love my job. I started out working there as a janitor, but I showed a lot of interest in the business, so I was able to work very closely with the founder, Mr. Byrd, and he taught me everything he knew. After a few years of hard work and dedication, I became a mortician. It has allowed me to afford a nice lifestyle. And just a few months ago, I was able to get my first apartment. So, I must admit I'm a little proud of what I've accomplished."

"Is that so? Well, I do say. Sounds to me like you're living the good life."

"I guess you could say that. I'm especially happy with my new place. I just got some new furniture in, but it could use a woman's touch here and there. Hey, you should come by one day and take a look at the place. See if you can sprinkle some of your womanly magic dust on it and make it a little better."

I wasn't quite sure how to respond to his invitation. "Maybe."

"Well, if you're not in a rush to get home, I live just a couple of miles away. You can swing by and take a look at it after we leave here, if you like."

I didn't respond, and I think he could sense my hesitation.

"Oh, I didn't mean to assume anything, Elizabeth. I'm sorry. I don't want to make you feel uncomfortable. I know you don't know me from a bar of soap, and here I am asking you to come to my apartment. Forgive me, please."

For fear that my hesitation would turn him away, I quickly gave him a better answer. "Oh, no. I can stop by for a few seconds and take a look at the place. I have my own vehicle, so I can just follow you there."

We finished our milkshakes. He paid the tab, and we left. The apartment building where he lived was a very nice, red brick, three-story building with two large trees flanking the walkway to the entrance. I pulled up in my car right behind his on the street. Just as I turned off the engine, he was at my car door, opening it up for me. For some reason, that impressed me. He was a definite gentleman.

He held out his arm for me to take it, and we walked up to the entrance and to his apartment on the first floor. He had a nicely furnished apartment, but there were no pictures on the walls or any decorative elements other than a huge array of various potted plants under the window in his living room. He definitely needed to add a few things to make it feel homey. But all in all, I liked it. He stood there in the middle of the room beaming with pride.

"What do you think?"

"I like it. It's very nice. As a matter of fact, I know just the thing for that wall behind the sofa. You need a large oil painting with some colors of green, blue, and such. It would really go nicely with the furniture."

"Yes! Yes. See, I knew you would be able to give me a few ideas. You look like a lady who can see things for what they are and figure out a way to add beauty to it."

I felt myself blushing, so I turned away. "Well, I guess I just know how to recognize the potential in things."

"I guess you do."

"Well, I need to be heading home. My godmother will be wondering where I am."

He reached out to grab my hand. "Elizabeth, may I see you again?"

"Yes. I would like that."

A couple of weeks following, Arnold and I met at a park where we sat, talked, and got to know each other a little better. Another time, we met at a local diner. I found myself starting to have a particular fondness for him. He was such a gentleman and very attentive, but I still had a little bit of an emotional guard up because of my past experiences. I was hopeful that he would continue to be kind and easygoing with me. This would surely allow me time to feel more at ease with the notion of allowing things to progress with him.

One Saturday afternoon, he had the day off from work, so he asked me to meet him at his apartment again so that I could help him figure out the perfect spots to hang up some other paintings that I suggested he purchased. He mentioned to me that he would be off for the entire day and would really like it if I could spend the day with him. I wasn't totally sold on the idea, so I told him that I would be able to come by just for a couple of hours but I had some errands to run for my godmother afterward.

It was early in the afternoon when I arrived at his apartment. He was inside with music playing on his record player, and he was preparing a light afternoon meal. The aroma of the food and the image of a man cooking was so nostalgic for me. It reminded me of my daddy in the kitchen cooking when I was a little girl.

He invited me to take a seat on the sofa, and he brought me a tall, cool glass of lemonade. I sat back and laid my pocketbook on the sofa next to me so that I could thoroughly enjoy all the things that were stimulating my senses: the music, the aromas, the visual of him cooking, the refreshing sweet tartness of the lemonade... These were all the things that made me want to take it all in and enjoy that moment.

"I trust you've been enjoying this beautiful weather we've been having today."

After taking a sip of lemonade, I licked my lips and looked up at him as he stood in front of me, wiping his hands on a dish towel.

"Yes, I have. It's been a wonderful day thus far."

"Well, if you would indulge me, after we settle on where to hang these paintings, I'd like you to stay and have lunch with me before you leave."

"Sure. I think I can find the time to fit in a meal."

I was actually hoping he'd ask me to stay for a little while. I wanted to see if his food tasted as good as it smelled. He'd prepared a big pot of oxtail stew, along with some hot water corn bread, and it did not disappoint. It was absolutely delicious. After we ate, we found the perfect areas on his walls to hang his paintings. Once done, we took a seat together on the sofa and admired their beauty. I was so pleased and satisfied with the way everything was going, but I knew that I had to be leaving soon.

"Well, Arnold, I hate to eat and run, but I really do need to be going."

He reached over and lightly touched my wrist. "Wait, don't go yet. I just want to enjoy your company a few minutes more."

He then reached over and laid his arm across the back of the sofa and scooted a little closer toward me. I felt my heart beginning to race. I knew that I liked this man, but I wasn't sure in that moment if I was ready to show him. As I was having this debate in my head, he leaned in closer and lightly touched my face to turn it toward his. He then looked me dead in my eyes and told me how beautiful he thought I was. I guess I zoned out because a few seconds later, he was kissing me on my neck and started working his way around to the other side of my neck.

I pulled back and whispered, asking him to wait. His kisses felt good, but I wasn't ready to go where he was trying to take me. He then used the weight of his body to slowly ease me down to lie flat on the sofa. My heart started racing faster, and I was thinking that maybe he didn't hear me tell him to wait. So, I said it a little louder.

"Wait, Arnold. I'm not ready for this. I'm sorry." He didn't respond. So, I said it again and louder. "Arnold, wait. Please!"

At that moment, I had a flashback to what happened to me in the back of that taxicab in Tennessee and at the hands of that bastard restaurant owner, and fear started to rise up from my feet to my chest. I was torn as to what to do. I liked Arnold, and I didn't want to react too intensely, but I wanted him to understand that I wasn't ready. I wanted him to stop!

He didn't stop. Arnold forced himself on me right there on his sofa, in front of the beautiful paintings we had hung together while the jazz song "Leap for Love" by Dutch Wellington played on the record player. I didn't scream. I didn't fight. I just lay there while silent tears streamed down my cheeks, and I let the music take me to a faraway place in my mind.

When his silent violation was over, the music kept playing. He stood up and kissed me on my forehead as if he was sealing his defilement of my body with a sweet tender kiss, as if he felt like what he had just done to me was an intimate and consensual act between two lovers.

Without any direct eye contact and in a smooth, low-pitched tone, he said to me, "I need to go take a shower. I'm certain you know your way out."

I waited until he left the room to rearrange my undergarments, grab my pocketbook, and leave. I never saw Arnold again after that day. I never returned to that ice cream parlor where we met. And I never wanted to hear that song by Dutch Wellington ever again.

At that point in my life, I was broken. I had been hurt more than anyone should ever be. I had decided that I would just keep my focus on me and those in my life who actually loved me, which were Mother Walton and Marla. I didn't want to have anything to do with a man anytime soon. I knew that I had to find some inner strength to get past all the devastation that was my life for the past few years. I knew that there was something better waiting for me out there in the world, but I just had to be settled in the Lord and let him guide my steps. If I were to ever find any true love with a good man, it would certainly need to be one that God had for me. Until then, I was completely done with it all.

After another full year and turning twenty years old, I decided that it was time for me to reset my focus. I was determined to find peace in my life and in my relationship with the Lord. I also found comfort in my many conversations about life and God with Mother Walton. She was the one consistent person in my life that I felt I could confide in and gain true insight from. She was so wise and so unbelievably kind.

During the time that I lived with her, she didn't allow me to pay her. So, I discovered a way to show her my appreciation by taking it upon myself to do minor repairs and keep things neat and clean around the house. I had gotten so good with fixing things that I felt confident enough to knock down a wall between the living room and a small study on the main floor of the house.

She had been talking for months about how she wanted it done but couldn't afford to pay anyone. So, one day I decided I was going to take care of it for her. Once the wall was down, I cleaned up all the dust and debris, and made repairs to seal up the exposed portions of the wall. The next step was to freshen up the walls with a new coat of paint. I spent three full days painting out that entire space, walls and ceiling, armed with only a ladder and horsehair paintbrush.

Mother Walton was so appreciative and pleased with my work that she cooked up a feast of food, enough to feed an army, and invited some folks from the church over, including the pastor. Marla came by too. We all sat around eating, laughing, and enjoying the food and fellowship in the new improved space I created with my very own hands.

From that moment on, Mother Walton decided to invite some of the people from the church over for dinner almost every Sunday, at least during the warmer months. She didn't want folk tracking in snow during the winter. She was very particular about keeping her house neat and clean. So, during the winter, it was mainly just me and her, and sometimes Marla would come by, and every so often, the pastor would come over and have dinner with us as well.

During a cold day in early December, I was bringing in the mail and saw a letter addressed to Mother Walton from Detroit, Michigan. It was amid all the postcards and telegrams that were being sent to her for the holidays. Mother Walton was very well known in the COGIC church and the community, so it was nothing strange to see a bunch of mail for her. But this letter from Detroit stuck out to me because the penmanship on the envelope was so nice, and the sender was a man named Joshua Roman. I couldn't help but wonder who this person was and how he knew Mother Walton.

When I handed her the stack of mail, I made sure the letter was on top in hopes that she would make notice of it and open it up right there in front of me. But she just took the stack and laid it on the kitchen table next to her cup of coffee. I was so curious to know who this mystery man was. So, I decided to make myself a cup of coffee and sit right there at the kitchen table with her while she read her mail.

"Ooh wee! Look at all of this mail. So many postcards and tele-grams. I don't know which to read first."

"Well, maybe start with that letter on top. Whoever wrote that has some lovely handwriting, huh?"

"Why, yes, they certainly, do… Oh, this is from Uncle Joshua."

She ripped open the envelope and began to read it.

"He's saying he wants to come visit, after the holidays. Oh my. Now that would be lovely. He's actually one of my favorite uncles. We're only a few years apart, so we're quite close. I'd love to see him.

I'm going to write him back right away and let him know that I'll be expecting his visit soon."

"Oh that's nice, Mother Walton. I never seen you this excited about family coming to visit."

"Well, Joshua is a special somebody! He's the sweetest, kindest, most caring man I know. And he's handsome too! Ha ha! Uncle Joshua...Lord, have mercy. I sure do miss seeing him. I wonder if he's still driving that powder blue Chrysler Airflow. Matter of fact, that was the last time I saw him when he drove it all the way up here from Detroit. He had just purchased it, and he came here for my aunt Verdi Mae's funeral. That sho' was a pretty vehicle. Anyway, it'll be so nice to see Uncle Joshua again."

*****

It was a crisp clear day in February, and Mother Walton was in the kitchen baking her famous cinnamon pinwheels with the expectation of her uncle Joshua's arrival at any time. I loved those cinnamon pinwheels so much and loved to assist her with baking them because I knew I would have first selection of the biggest and best ones.

Just as she was putting the pinwheels into the oven, there was a knock at the door, followed by the door buzzer. Mother Walton slammed the oven door shut and snatched off her apron as she quickly made her way to the front door. I followed right behind her with eager anticipation of bearing first witness of her beloved Uncle Joshua.

She opened the door and welcomed him in. He was nothing like I had imagined, but as Mother Walton had said, he was handsome. He was tall with a slim build. He looked to be in his early fifties. He had medium-toned brown skin and high cheekbones. His hair was very curly and soft looking, with small flecks of gray. It was cut low on the sides with a little extra height on the top and a side part. He greeted Mother Walton with a big smile and wide-open arms.

"Uncle Joshua, come on in here and take a load off. It's certainly good to see you!"

"Well, it's good to be seen." He shot a look over at me and motioned his hand in my direction. "Who is this young lady?"

"Pardon me. This is Elizabeth Davidson. She is one of the young ladies from my church, and she's boarding here. Elizabeth, this is my uncle Joshua Roman.

I extended my hand to him. "Pleased to meet you, Mr. Roman."

"My pleasure as well, and you don't have to call me Mr. Roman. Joshua suits me just fine."

As he made his way into the living room from the entryway, he took a look around, surveying the room.

"Norma, this room looks different. It looks bigger…"

"Oh, well, I owe that to Elizabeth. She knocked down this wall and painted the whole room all by herself."

"You're kidding me! You mean to tell me that this pretty young lady did all that by herself? Well, I'm impressed!" He turned to look at me. "Who taught you how to do this?"

I was beaming with pride and offered a corresponding response. "I taught myself. I just knew what needed to be done, and I did it."

"Well, slap my back and call me Sally! I am impressed. You did a wonderful job…a wonderful job!"

I was grinning from ear to ear. "Thank you."

"Uncle Joshua, may I take your hat and coat? Elizabeth, would you take his suitcase to the back bedroom, please?"

"Sure thing." I was delighted to do so.

As Joshua handed me his small suitcase, I noticed a unique ring he wore on his right hand. It was a large silver ring with a black flat-faced stone that appeared to have an Indian head carving in the middle of the stone. It caught my eye, and I wanted to get a closer look at it, but I didn't want to be obvious. But he noticed I was looking.

"I acquired this ring from my uncle before he died. He was part Cherokee. He gave it to me when I was a young man back in my hometown of Little Rock, Arkansas. It's very near and dear to my heart."

"Very nice. I've never seen a ring like that before. It's very different."

Mother Walton chimed in, "Come on in the kitchen, Uncle Joshua. I made a pot of coffee, and I have some cinnamon pinwheels baking in the oven. They should be just about ready."

I took his suitcase to his room and thought that I'd retreat upstairs. I was thinking that I'd just let him have first pick of the pinwheels since he was company. But just as I was about to head up, Mother Walton called me into the kitchen. They were both sitting at the kitchen table, chuckling.

Joshua looked up at me standing in the doorway and said, "Elizabeth, Norma told me how you like to have first selection of these little beauties when they're fresh out the oven. And I feel it would be wrong for me to disrupt the order of things around here."

I playfully cut my eyes over at her. "Oh, really? She told you that, huh?"

We all chuckled a bit more. I was a little embarrassed that she'd told him that. But I was also a little glad that he was thoughtful enough to allow me to make my selection first. I sheepishly offered my gratitude and made my way over to the stove where they were cooling off and chose the one that looked most appealing to me.

Again, I was about to make my retreat when Mother Walton welcomed me to take a seat with them and enjoy a cup of hot coffee as well. I was surprised that she invited me to stay and talk. Usually when she has company, other than when she holds large dinners, I'm asked to be excused as if I were a child. But she actually invited me to take a seat right there at the table with them. I was excited and nervous at the same time. For the first time, I was being allowed to engage in conversation with her and her company.

We sat at the kitchen table for what seemed like hours as they shared stories about their family. I learned a lot about Mother Norma Walton. Of course, I knew that she wasn't in the church her entire life. I mean I know that she wasn't born an Evangelist. But it was certainly refreshing to hear that she had a regular upbringing just like me.

It was also very interesting to know that Joshua served in World War I, seeing as how it was only about seven years since World War II ended in 1945. He told stories about growing up poor in Little

Rock and how he didn't really know his actual birth date because he was born on a farm way out in the country by the hands of a midwife. And it wasn't normal practice for black folk in that set of circumstances to be issued a birth certificate. He knew that he was born in the month of January in 1899, which would put him at age fifty-three. But he didn't know his actual date of birth.

He also mentioned that he was once married to a lady who had three teenage children from a previous marriage. But unfortunately, she died of a heart attack not long after receiving the news that two of them were killed in a horrible car accident. I wanted to ask more about it, but he was visibly upset recalling it, so he quickly changed the subject.

He mentioned that he was currently working at a major automotive corporation and had a few years to go before he could retire. He talked about how he loved living in the city of Detroit and wanted Mother Walton to come there to visit him for a change. He assured her that she'd love the city.

As the evening hours drew closer, Mother Walton and Joshua decided to suspend the conversation and trips down memory lane so that he could freshen up and get a little rest before supper. By this time, Marla had stopped by to drag me out to go dress shopping with her for a date with Woody that she was getting prepared for. I didn't care for Woody too much because he was an outright jackass! But Marla loved him, so I tolerated him.

When Marla arrived, just as she would normally do, she popped her head into the kitchen to say hello to Mother Walton. She saw that we had company, so she offered a greeting to Joshua as well, and we were on our way out the door.

"Girl, who is that fine 'mane' sitting up in y'alls kitchen?" She pronounced man as if it had the letter e at the end of it.

"Oh, that's Mother Walton's uncle visiting her from Detroit."

"Uncle? You say he's her uncle? They look about the same age."

"Yeah, they're just two years apart."

Marla had a devilish grin. "Hmmm. Well, how long he's staying for?"

"Just a few days. He's actually only stopping here on his way down to his hometown of Little Rock to visit some of their relatives for a few extra days, and then he'll be headed back up to Detroit sometime next week."

"Well, you certainly know a lot about his plans, don't you?"

I rolled my eyes and waved her off. "Girl, you sho' do know how to keep up mess! Come on, let's go get to these stores before they close. You know you always like starting out late to take care of your business."

We made our way to the main shopping district and ran in and out of several stores before stumbling on a dress for her to wear to her special date with Woody. She was so excited and said that she believed he was going to ask her to marry him. I tried my best to seem genuinely happy for her, but it was difficult. I just knew that he was bad news. He just didn't treat her right. I know that I had my share of being mistreated by men, but at least I didn't choose to find myself in a bona fide relationship with a man who mistreated me and put me down every chance he got. Marla just didn't know her real worth.

Mother Walton used to tell me that I was more of a friend to Marla than she was to me and that she showed signs of jealousy toward me, but I didn't see that. I just knew that Marla didn't have that inner strength that she needed to be her own person without having a man in her life. She teased me for getting rid of Arnold so quickly, but she didn't know the details of what happened, and I wasn't about to tell anybody about it, not even Marla. She was always clowning around and teasing me about things, but I believed that it was just part of her personality to pick with folks. She thought she was funny, but I just put up with it because I loved her crazy tail like a sister.

The following night, Marla and Woody went out on their date to a local black-owned nightclub, and he indeed proposed to her. She was so excited to come and tell me all about it the following day. And once again, I had to pretend to be happy for her. I did, however, let her know that I wished her the very best and that I'd be there to support her, no matter what.

*****

It was the day before it was time for Joshua to continue his travel south to Arkansas, and he was sitting on the living room sofa reading the Bible. I tried to walk past so as not to disturb him, but he noticed me. He spoke and asked me if I knew where he could go to pick up some fish because he wanted to cook us some fish, okra, and baked sweet potatoes tonight before he set out on the road tomorrow. I told him about the fish market not too far from where we lived, and he put his Bible down on the sofa next to him, reached into his pocket for his keys, and announced that he'd be back shortly to get started cooking.

Once he left, I tiptoed over to the sofa to sneak a look at what scripture he was reading. It was turned to the book of 1 Corinthians, chapter 13, which speaks on the importance of us having charity (love). It made me feel a little bit sorry for him. I knew that he must have loved his deceased wife and stepchildren because of the way he recalled the story of how they died. I couldn't imagine going through something like that. I knew what it was like to lose a mother, but to lose almost your entire family had to be the worst pain ever. At that moment, I decided I would keep Joshua in my prayers to God for his heart to be healed and that he would hopefully find love again.

Just a little while later, he returned and cooked the meal, and Mother Walton made it back home from a meeting down at the church. Joshua had the house smelling so good! We all sat down and enjoyed what Joshua had prepared. He even baked a pound cake that made me want to do backflips because it was so good!

After I cleared the dishes from the table, he and Mother Walton retired to the living room to spend a few more hours together before bedtime. I stayed in the kitchen and washed the dishes. Then I went to my room so that they could continue talking. Before I went to sleep, I made sure to say a prayer for Joshua.

After a few weeks had passed since Joshua left, I wondered if he had made it back to Detroit safely. Mother Walton hadn't made any mention of it, so I decided to ask. She was in the kitchen, as she normally was, so I yelled out to her from the living room.

"Mother Walton, do you know if your uncle made it back to Detroit okay?"

"Oh, yes! He sent a postcard last week thanking me for the hospitality, and he mentioned how much he enjoyed his stay." There was a slight pause, then she poked her head out from the kitchen and winked at me. "He even said how much of a pleasure it was meeting you."

Then she popped her head back into the kitchen to continue with whatever it was she was doing in there. I was glad to hear that he was back home and that he enjoyed his stay here. But I honestly was even more pleased to know that he made mention of me in his note. For some strange reason, I felt compelled to be concerned about this man's well-being. Maybe it was the Lord leading me to be mindful of him for whatever reason. So, every night, I included him in my list of people and things to pray for.

For a whole six months straight, I prayed for this man until one day, I questioned if I should stop because I was starting to become very curious about him. I not only wanted to know how he was, but I wanted to know more about *him*. I decided to talk with Mother Walton about what I was feeling because I knew there would be no judgment from her on the matter. So, I went to her room and knocked on her door.

She was sitting up in her bed, reading. "Come on in, baby. What's going on?"

I went on to explain to her that I had been including Joshua in my nightly prayers, along with the list of all the other people and things.

"I can't seem to reconcile why I'm so concerned about him. I even thought that maybe it's best if I just stop praying for him because of it. Is this normal? I don't want my focus to shift in a direction that is not of the Lord."

"Baby, who said loving someone is not of the Lord?"

"Oh, no. I don't love him. I'm just concerned that's all."

"Elizabeth, I've been around long enough to know when a woman has feelings for a man. And from what you are sharing with me, it's quite obvious to me that you have caught feelings for him, and that is perfectly fine. He is a God-fearing man and a good-hearted man. Now, I'm not saying you're looking to run away and marry the man, but don't think I don't know what caring for a man looks like."

"But, Mother Walton, he's thirty-some years older than me. And he's your uncle. What would that look like, me wanting after a man that's old enough to be my father? Ha! I just wanted to come and talk out these thoughts I was warring with about his well-being and perhaps me spending too much time being concerned about him. Perhaps I need to limit my prayers for him because Lord knows I ain't got no business bothering myself with the notion of catching feelings for a man more than twice my age."

She looked at me over the rim of her glasses. "Okay. You just keep on telling yourself that and see how far it gets you. Good night, and pull up my door, dear."

"Yes, ma'am."

I walked down the hall to my room, feeling more confused than I was before, thinking maybe that she could see something I refused to see. I decided that I would hold off on praying for him at least for tonight. But he was in my dreams that night. I couldn't shake this man from my head!

After about another month or so of battling with myself, I decided to put pen to paper and just drop him a short letter in the mail to let him know that the Lord had placed him in my spirit to keep him in my prayers and to just wish him well. There was certainly no harm in that.

Dear Joshua,

I hope this letter finds you well. Ever since your visit here to St. Louis, it has been impressed upon my heart to hold you up in prayer before God. I just wanted to reach out to you and let you know that you must be loved by the Lord because he's got me praying for you nightly! I just wanted to share this scripture with you (1 John 4:7–11), and it is my hope that you meditate on it often so that it brings you continued comfort and encouragement.

Sincerely,
Elizabeth

I stared down at what I had written, going over it a few times to make sure that it read properly and that there was nothing that could be read in between the lines. I didn't want this man thinking that I was attempting to seek him out in any way that was inappropriate.

A little time had gone by, and I didn't receive any response from my letter. I started to wonder if he even received it. Or maybe he received it but scoffed at it. At the point where I was just getting ready to give up on the hopes that he had received my letter, I received a response. The envelope had that same neat handwriting on it, and it was addressed to me! I tore it open and read every line.

Dear Elizabeth,

Thank you for the lovely letter you sent me. I must say I was a bit surprised to see a letter from you. Rest assured, all is well with me. I have been diligently working on the job every day and attending church every Sunday. I lead a rather simple life, not much to it at all. I really do appreciate the scripture you shared with me. It shows me that you are a woman that has a heart for God and his people. I guess I should also tell you that I have prayed for you a few times as well. You seem to be a wonderful young woman, and I am sure that there is a lot in store for you. Keep being a blessing to my niece and keep those encouraging scriptures coming!

Sincerely,
Joshua

Wait…was this an invitation to continue writing him? I think so. And so, I did. We wrote each other back and forth for almost a year.

Dear Elizabeth,

This Friday, I'll be traveling back to Little Rock to visit my brother, Rudolph. He's not doing too well. They say he has cancer and doesn't have much longer. Please, say a prayer for him. And say one for me as well. I know this is the time that the Church of God in Christ usually has their annual convention. And I'm sure Norma is away from home doing the Lord's work. But, please, be sure tell her about her uncle Rudolph so that she may keep him in her prayers also. It is my hope that I make it to him in time before his passing. I will let you and Norma know once I make it to Arkansas.

Love,
Joshua

My heart skipped a little bit when I read the closing to his letter, "Love, Joshua." But I didn't want to focus on that because the more pressing issue was the fact that his brother was gravely ill, and he was hurting. Mother Walton would be returning from the church convention soon, and I made sure to let her know when she returned. But by the time she made it back, we had received a telegram that Rudolph had passed away just two days prior to her return.

Three days later, Joshua stopped in St. Louis after the funeral on his way back to Detroit. He was understandably solemn and appeared to be quite exhausted. He wanted to rest overnight and head up north the next day. Mother Walton welcomed him in and sat with him in the living room while they both shed some tears and reminisced about Rudolph. I stayed out of sight for a while to allow them time. It was still early in the evening, but Mother Walton came upstairs for bed earlier than usual.

"Elizabeth, I'm going to bed, honey. Please, look after Uncle Joshua for me. Make sure he's all set and doesn't need anything before he retires to bed. I know he's awfully tired and will need some rest before he heads home tomorrow. Thank you, honey."

"Sure thing, Mother Walton. I've got things covered. Good night."

Right then, I went downstairs to check on him to see if he needed anything before going to his room. He was just sitting there on the sofa with his head in his hands, sobbing. I didn't know what to do. I was frozen. He slowly lifted his head and saw me standing there.

"I'm sorry."

My heart was breaking for him. "No, please don't apologize. He was your brother."

He lowered his head into his hands again and covered his face as if to hide the tears. I walked slowly over to the sofa, sat on the edge of the cushion, and extended my hand to lightly touch his shoulder in a sign of support. I wanted to comfort him but didn't know how exactly. I felt his shoulders lower as he let out a long sigh. We sat there for a few seconds before he spoke.

"Thank you."

"No need to thank me. I just hate to see anyone in pain. I know what it is to lose someone you love. It hurts like nothing you can describe."

"Yes, it does."

He reached over and touched my hand as he stood and straightened upright. "Well, I better be getting to bed so I can hit this road in the morning."

I stood up, facing him. He looked at me and offered a slight smile. I offered a quick one in return. I opened my arms to offer him a consoling embrace. He sniffed a time or two, which let me know he was still crying. I hugged him a little tighter and allowed him to feel that it was okay for him to freely express his pain. We stood there for a moment and slowly released our embrace. He thanked me again and said good night. I went back upstairs with my heart racing and breaking for him at the same time.

The next morning, I got up extra early to get myself together so that I could say goodbye to him as he set off on his way back to Detroit. I heard him and Mother Walton talking in the kitchen, so I rushed to the mirror to check my hair then made my way downstairs. His travel bag was at the door with his hat sitting on top. He looked so dapper when he wore that hat. Just as I rounded the bottom of the staircase, they were walking in my direction toward the front door.

The sight of him made my heart skip. I wasn't sure what it was I was feeling, but I knew that it was unlike any feeling I had ever felt. This man, thirty years my senior, was someone I felt connected to in a way that was unexplainable. It wasn't lust…but something deeper. Something of a certain substance I was not accustomed to.

He smiled at me, and I smiled back. Mother Walton stood there smiling too. I didn't know why she was smiling. It made me think that maybe they were talking about me over their morning cup of coffee. It made me wonder if she shared with him what I had shared with her. It made me hope that he didn't tell her about our embrace last night. Her smile made me more nervous than his! I stood there, frozen right in his path to the door.

"Lord, chile, move out the way so Uncle Joshua can get on his way back home."

Her words snapped me back. "Oh. Oh, yes, I'm sure you're ready to get going."

He looked at me and gave me a wink. "I wish I could stay longer, but I do need to get back."

Mother Walton reached down, picked up his hat, and handed it to him. "May God keep you and cover you on your journey home. May his angels encamp around you, and may you arrive to your destination safe and sound. In the precious name of our Lord and Savior. Amen."

She gave him a quick hug and stepped aside, allowing me to give my goodbye.

"Umm. Well, umm. I hate to see you go. I, umm…"

He interrupted with a slight chuckle. "I'll be fine. And thank you for being a shoulder to lean on. Thank you both. I'll be in touch."

Joshua stepped out the door onto the front porch, and Mother Walton said a final goodbye then walked back into the kitchen. I stepped out onto the porch with Joshua. He stepped backward, one foot down on the step behind him and one foot on the porch, putting us at eye level.

"Well, be safe, Joshua. And I hope to see you again soon."

"You will."

We both stood there in silence for a moment as if neither of us knew what to do or say next. I decided to give him a final hug goodbye. It lasted for only a second or two. As I released my embrace, my eyes met his. And I saw what could not be found in any other man's eyes. I saw goodness, meekness, and safety when I looked into his eyes. I felt and saw love when I looked into his eyes. I leaned in and took a little deeper gaze, and it was at that moment that I had no more fear. I leaned in a bit more with the full intention of planting a kiss on his cheek, and I felt free to do so. The warmth of his skin was like a kindle, like nothing I've ever felt before. I felt something rise in me like a warm ember ready to take flight.

After that day, Joshua and I wrote to each other almost every other week or so.

Dear Joshua,

I got caught in the rain today, and I thought about you. I was walking home when it started. I didn't bother to take cover or hurry along my way. I just let it wash over me. I was soaking wet and didn't care one bit because it reminded me of you and the way you make me feel. I took my time walking home. And I smiled all the way there covered in the pouring rain, wanting more of it, just as I want more of you.

Love,
Elizabeth

My Dear, Sweet Love,

I will be back in St. Louis in a few months, and I can't wait to see you. By the way, I received your letter today, and I could not seem to put it down. I never would have thought that our encounter would have developed this way. I have not been caught by surprise much in my life. You not only surprised me but you managed to surprise my heart! Never in a hundred years did I think that I would come to feel this way about anyone again. You are precious and sweet. You are a blessing beyond measure. You are lovely and loving. I thank the good Lord above for bringing you into my life. What started as a casual encounter quickly grew into a friendship. And from that, we have crossed over into something much more special.

Elizabeth, you are a true jewel that I will cherish for as long as you will allow. See you soon, my dear.

Love,
Joshua

It was the summer of 1953, and I would soon be turning twenty-two. I had great anticipation of Joshua coming back to St. Louis. I couldn't wait to see him. And when he came back, well, it was evident that he couldn't wait to see me either.

When he arrived, Mother Walton was out running errands. So, Joshua and I sat on the sofa in the front room talking and holding hands. I could tell that he was nervous. He was breathing deep and heavy and appeared to be preoccupied by something. I didn't press him. I figured a man of his age surely has things that occupy the mind that I would have no notion of. So, I simply ignored his peculiar behavior.

The few days Joshua spent in St. Louis were coming to an end, and once again, he would be headed back to Detroit. On his final evening in town, we went for a long walk, and on the way back to the house, we stopped to sit on a bench at the park up the street.

It was dusk and would be dark soon, so I wasn't too keen on stopping at this spot when we were just a few blocks away from the house. But he was insistent. He took a handkerchief from his pocket and wiped the sweat from his brow and then he took my hand. On that evening, Joshua profoundly confessed his love for me, got down on one knee, and pulled out a ring from his shirt pocket. Joshua Roman asked for my hand in marriage.

Although there was a lot to consider as it pertained to our age difference, I knew that he was a good man and that he would love and care for me like no other. I looked at him, and I didn't hesitate. I said yes. Before he left to return to Detroit, we decided that I would only stay in St. Louis a few more months before he would return for us to get married.

# CHAPTER FIVE

# Detroit, Here I Come

Mother Walton was overjoyed when I told her about Joshua's proposal, and she gushed over the ring. I know that she was happy for him, but I also know that she was truly happy for me as well. My best friend Marla was also very happy for me. In fact, she had a bit of news herself to share. She was pregnant with Woody's baby and was planning to get married at the courthouse by the end of the month. She wanted to do it before she started showing. I had to admit that her news was just as impactful but not as delightful. I couldn't stand Woody. He was a plum fool, and I could only see years of heartache ahead for her if she married that man.

Well, sure enough, just a week and a half later, Marla Filmore was the newly married Marla Eastern and two months pregnant. And three weeks after that, Marla showed up on Mother Walton's porch with a black eye from her new husband, and she was crying uncontrollably.

"Liz, he's cheating on me! How could he do that? I found a woman's glove on the floor of the car. So, I asked him whose glove it was. And he gone tell me it's mine. Like I don't know what's mine and what's not! So, when I questioned him again, he started yelling and cursing, telling me not to question him. Talking 'bout 'Do you know who you're talking to? I'm Woody Eastern! Don't nobody question Woody Eastern!' Then he hauled off and slapped me across my face. I got out the car and ran up to our apartment. He threw the car into park and followed behind me, yelling, 'You hear me, Marla! You don't question me! Don't nobody question me!' So, when we got into the apartment, I picked up the phone to call the police, and he snatched the receiver away from me and hit me in the face with it. Elizabeth, I don't know what to do! He got up and went to work the next morning like nothing ever happened."

With each detail she gave, the madder I got. I wanted to go catch that fool and beat the life out of him. How could a man put his hands on his wife, his pregnant wife at that? I told Marla what she should do to him the next time he decides he wants to manhandle her.

About a month later, I got a call from Marla. She was down at the hospital. I was so upset that I dropped what I was doing and drove there, doing well over the speed limit. When I arrived, I rushed in and spotted her sitting in a chair in the waiting area. I hurried over to her and sat down next to her and took a second to catch my breath before I could speak.

"Marla, are you okay? Is the baby okay?"

She was holding her head in her hands and crying.

"Marla, sweetie, are you hurt?"

Her crying changed a little. She raised her head and looked at me with tears streaming down her face. And her crying quickly turned into laughter.

"Nah, I ain't hurt, but he damn sure is."

In astonishment, I replied, "What? You say he's hurt? What you mean he's hurt?"

"I mean just that. I took your advice and got back at that bastard. He came in drunk last night and wanted to start some mess. I kept asking him to leave me alone, but he just kept on at me. So, while he was talking, I put a pot of water on the stove. And he kept right on yelling and threatening to beat my ass. He said he had a bat in the trunk of the car and he was going to go get it. So, he left out the apartment and down the back stairs. While he was out getting his bat, I got the pot off the stove and waited for his ass at the top of the steps. Liz, I wasn't about to let him get me again. I was ready for him this time. I waited until he got halfway up the stairs, and I tossed that pot of hot water right on him. He lucky it only scalded him on his chest and thighs."

She looked at me with the most serious look, and I stared back at her, wide-eyed, with my hand over my mouth. Then we both burst out in laughter! After that incident, things were a bit more peaceful between Marla and Woody. But I wasn't too hopeful it would last long.

Within the next few weeks, I had made my way across town to visit my father to let him know that I was engaged to be married and would be moving to Detroit next year. By this time, Nellie had put our father in a nursing home because of his medical problems. She didn't want to take care of him herself. She was just too evil and selfish to care for anyone other than herself. Daddy didn't seem to care one way or another when I told him the news. He just sat there in his bed with his hands on his lap, staring off into the distance and nodding yes or no whenever I asked him a question. I kissed my daddy's cheek and cut my visit a little short. I promised him I'd be back to visit with him again soon. He just said okay, all while staring off into the distance.

Joshua and I were married in St. Louis the day before Thanksgiving in 1954 in Mother Walton's home. It was a beautiful and private ceremony. We stayed a few days in St. Louis and made one more visit to say goodbye to my father. Then I made it my business to say a farewell to other family and friends. Afterward, I packed up all my things and we headed to Detroit.

I was so excited to start my new life with the man I loved. A few months after we wed, I became pregnant with my first child, and had my beautiful baby boy in the fall of 1955. Joshua Roman Jr. was the light of my life. He brought me more joy than my heart could hold. It gave me purpose to be his mother.

Joshua Roman Sr. and I were living in a small apartment just off Woodward Avenue. We were somewhat comfortable, but I must admit that I thought things would be a little better financially than they were. I honestly thought that since my husband had held a long-term job at the automotive corporation and was nearing retirement, he would've had a nest egg set aside. But I soon learned after marrying him that he had suffered a horrible financial loss during his first marriage. It turns out that the story he shared with me a couple of years ago about the horrible automobile accident involving his step-children resulted in him being sued by the other party because he was the owner of the car. He lost everything he owned behind that ordeal—his house, his savings, everything. So, needless to say, it was a bit of a surprise to learn this information after we were married. But it didn't matter to me too much. I loved him regardless of how much money he had or didn't have. I loved him because of who he was and how he treated me.

I took pride in caring for my husband, my baby, and my home. Although I kept a tidy apartment, I made it my business to do a routine, detailed cleaning each Saturday. While cleaning up one afternoon, I received a phone call from Marla. Once again, she was crying, and I could hear her now two-year-old daughter, Brenda, crying in the background. I could tell from the sobbing and the desperation in her voice that it had something to do with that ignorant ass, Woody Eastern.

"Elizabeth, I just can't take it anymore. I have to leave him. He has really lost it this time. He accused me of cheating on him and jumped on me again. I fought him off, but I can't continue to live like this. And I can't continue to let my child see me living like this. I don't know what to do. I have some family in Kalamazoo, Michigan, that say they would be willing to take Brenda, but they ain't gonna allow me to stay there because they think he'll track me down and cause problems for them. So, I don't know what to do."

My heart was breaking for my friend, and as I held the phone, listening to her, Joshua saw the sadness on my face. He asked me what was going on. I put my hand over the receiver and quickly told him.

"It's Marla. Woody jumped on her again. She needs to leave him. Her people in Kalamazoo said they'll let her daughter stay with them but not her. Marla needs a place to stay."

"Liz, just tell her she can come stay here until she figures things out."

Relieved that he had offered, I let out a big sigh and removed my hand from the phone.

"Marla, where is Woody now?"

She replied, "I don't know. He left outa here drunk. Ain't no telling where he went."

"Okay. Well, Marla, you pack up all that you have right now and get a train ticket to Detroit as soon as you can. Once you get here, I'll drive you to Kalamazoo to take Brenda to your cousin's house, and you can stay here with us."

"Oh, no, Elizabeth, I don't want to be a burden to you and Joshua. I won't have no way to pay you or help with food."

"Marla, you're like a sister to me. If I eat, you eat. Don't worry about paying us anything. Just come on!"

Marla arrived the next day with Brenda in tow. Joshua and I drove her two hours to Kalamazoo to drop off Brenda, and then we turned around and came back to Detroit with Marla. We had a two-bedroom apartment, but since the other room was being used by our son, I made her a spot on the sofa. The plan was for her to stay with us until she was able to get a job and get on her feet.

Unfortunately, Woody found out that she was with me and started to call every day, scorning her and insisting that she come back home. He said that he wanted her and Brenda back where they belong, with him. He accused her of being a horrible mother and even went so far as to suggest that she, Joshua, and I must be all sleeping together. I had just about had it with his antics. I couldn't understand how she ever saw anything good enough in him to want to align herself with him in the first place.

One day, he called while Joshua was at work and Marla was out looking for work. I was at home with the baby, and the phone just kept ringing and ringing. I knew it was him, so I didn't want to pick up. But I felt like maybe if I gave him a piece of my mind and told his ass off good enough, he would stop calling.

"Hello?"

"Put Marla on the phone, please."

"She ain't here, Woody. And you're gonna stop calling here, disrupting my home. You ain't nothing but a broke-down drunk loser, with no respect for yourself or nobody else. You need to quit calling here and leave Marla alone. She don't want your drunk, ignorant ass no way!"

He responded in an extremely loud and indignant tone. "Who in the hell do you think you're talking to? That's *my* wife! And as long as I'm black and living, ain't no woman gonna tell me nothing about me or how I handle my business. Marla belongs *to* me and *with* me! You hear me? You ain't running nothing. Matter of fact, I know what to do for you. I can handle you all the way from St. Louis. I promise you that. You done messed with the wrong one! You have Marla call me when she gets in!"

That jackass slammed down the phone in my ear before I could say anything else. I wanted him to know I wasn't afraid of him. I could take his little scrawny tail and twist him up like a pretzel with no problem. He didn't intimidate me in the least. Unfortunately, I think he was just too much of a fool to even consider how it was his actions that was negatively affecting his family. He was the for real kind of crazy.

A few hours later, Marla made it back to the apartment in a bit of a funk because she had not yet found work. I didn't bother to inform her that Woody had called because I didn't want to upset her any more than she already was. I was feeding the baby when the phone rang again. Marla jumped at the phone to answer it.

I could hear Woody's voice coming through the receiver. He was yelling and cursing to the top of his voice. She was just sitting there, obviously frustrated and literally holding her mouth to keep herself from yelling back at him. I figured that she was doing that because I was sitting there with the baby. So, I excused myself to my bedroom so she could feel free to give it to him. While I was in the bedroom, I could hear her yelling and cursing him out. After a minute or two, it got quiet. I strained to listen, but I couldn't hear anything but a light mumbling. I pressed my ear to the bedroom door to try to hear a little better. Then I heard the apartment door open and close.

I looked over at the clock on the wall and realized it must've been Joshua coming in from work. I went out to the front room, and no one was there. I looked in the kitchen. No one. I went to the apartment door to look out into the hallway. No one. I was confused.

Why did Marla leave without saying anything? I closed the door and sat on the sofa with the baby. About five minutes later, Joshua came in. I asked him if he had seen Marla leaving, and he hadn't. I figured she must've just needed to get some air to cool off from the heated conversation with Woody.

It was four hours later when Marla made a quiet reentry. Joshua and I were getting ready for bed. I heard the apartment door creak open gradually, and the floorboards squeak as she slowly stepped in. I didn't bother to call out to her or go into the living room. I assumed that she likely wanted to just go to bed and forget that today's events ever happened. And I understood totally.

The next morning, Joshua was up getting ready for work, and I was putting on a pot of coffee in the kitchen. Marla was just a few feet away, asleep on the sofa, so I was trying my best to be very quiet. Joshua left out the front door, and I went back to my room to lie down a little longer while the baby was still sleep. It was midmorning when I finally got up, and surprisingly, the baby was lying peacefully in his crib. I was headed to the bathroom to wash up and start my day when I heard Marla call my name. She was sitting on the sofa, fully dressed, and had her travel bag right next to her at the foot of the sofa.

"Elizabeth, I just want to let you know that I'll be leaving for the bus station. I'm going to Kalamazoo to stay with my family."

I was a little thrown off by her sudden announcement. "What? Why?"

"I just need to be with my baby and family."

I had a feeling that there was more to it, but I didn't press the issue. "Okay. I understand. Just let me know when you need to be at the bus station, and I'll take you."

"Oh, no. I called a cab. But I thank you for everything."

And with that, a few minutes later, Marla was walking out my door and down the stairs to the cab. She did make it to Kalamazoo. But her cousin called me two days later to tell me that Woody drove all the way from St. Louis and got her and her daughter and took them back to St. Louis with him.

I was too outdone. How could she be so forgiving of him? What was the point of going through all the trouble of saying she wanted to leave him, catching a train all the way here to Detroit, having me and my husband pack up our baby and drive a total of four hours to Kalamazoo and back to take her child to her family and allowing her stay here with us, all for her to decide to go back to him? I just didn't understand. A few weeks later, I received a letter from Marla that explained everything.

Elizabeth,

I didn't want to tell you this while I was in your home with you and your baby. But I thought it best that I at least let you know why I left so suddenly. Woody told me that you and him slept together back when you were living here in St. Louis.

Now I don't know for sure if this is true, but I can't bear to even think that you would be so bold as to do something like that to me. I had to leave and get my mind together. I can't say for sure one way or the other. But honestly, I can't imagine why he would just make something like that up.

I don't know, Elizabeth. I just don't know what to think. We have been friends for about five years now, and I thought you were a true friend. And maybe you are. Maybe he's a horrible person and a liar. But until I can sort things out, I think it's for the best that we take time away from each other for a while.

If this is true, I'll ask God to help me forgive you. And if I'm wrong, I hope you can forgive me.

Marla

Reading that letter broke my heart. I couldn't believe that Marla would actually believe that I might be capable of doing something like that to her. I would never sleep with any man she was interested in, and especially not a full-fledged fool like Woody Eastern! Maybe Mother Walton was right all along about Marla. Maybe it was true that I was more of a friend to her than she was to me. And I figured that if she was willing to let that fool come between us, then they deserved each other.

It was now clear to me that when Woody said that he could "handle me" all the way from St. Louis and that I was messing with the wrong one, I guess this was what he meant. He conjured up this horrible lie about me and him sleeping together, and Marla believed it.

It was then and there that I decided I would focus on my family and not worry about Marla. I had decided that if she ever came to her senses, I'd consider working things out with her. But until that happened, it was full steam ahead for my life.

After about two years, I heard from one of Marla's relatives that she had divorced Woody and moved to Kalamazoo with family until she could get on her feet. I wanted to reach out to her and check on her and her daughter, but I decided that I would let things lie where they were for now until either she reached out to me or I got up enough nerve to actually call her.

I would often speak with her cousin and get reports from her on Marla's well-being, but if I had it my way, me and Marla would be hanging like wet clothes again if things were right between us.

I tried to create new friendships with people in Detroit, but they kept disappointing. Either they were dishonest or users. I didn't have much, but I would have no problems helping others. I tried to befriend a lady who was my hairdresser. She seemed very personable and sweet. She was fun to talk to, and I liked that about her. One day while she was doing my hair, she asked if she could borrow fifty dollars from me. I was hesitant at first. I considered my financial situation in my response to her.

"Let me be honest with you, I don't have money to give away. If you can promise me that you'll have this back to me by the first of the month, then I'll loan it to you. I have bills that will be due, so I mean it when I say I need it back by the first of the month."

"You have my word. I don't play when it comes to other people's money. I'll have it back to you by next week, as a matter of fact. And since I do hair almost every day, I can get this back to you easily. I just got behind on my car payment because I was helping my brother out. So, after I do a few clients, I'll be able to pay you back next week for sure."

A week went by, and no word from her. Then another week, no word. The first of the month was just a couple of days away, so I called up the hair salon where she worked, and the receptionist said that she wasn't in. The next day, I got myself together, put my 38 Special in my purse, and made my way down to the hair salon. When I got there, the receptionist asked me if I had an appointment, and I explained to her that I was there on personal business.

For the life of me, I can't remember my hairdresser's name now, but I sure do remember her face and the way she looked when she saw me standing at the receptionist's desk asking for her. When we made eye contact, I started walking in her direction. She hadn't started her workday at that point. As she was setting up, I took a seat in a chair right next to her station. I politely opened my purse and showed her a flash view of my pistol.

"Since you didn't bother to pay me my money as promised, I'm gonna sit right here and collect my money as you collect yours."

She looked at me as if I was crazy and started trembling and crying.

I whispered to her, "I wouldn't have to do this if you had just kept your word. I told you good that I didn't have no money to just give away, and you told me that you'd have my money back to me within a week. Here it is two weeks later, and I ain't heard from you. I need my money back today, and I ain't leaving here until I get it. So, you need to dry up your tears and get yourself together to serve your clients and make enough money to pay me what's mine. After that, I don't care what the hell you do."

I sat there in that chair next to her station and placed one of my hands slightly inside my purse and the other hand on top of my purse as a reminder to her of what was inside. Then I collected my money from her after each client paid for their services. Once I got all fifty dollars from her, I promptly got up from my seat, zipped up my purse, and informed her that our friendship was over and not to expect me back as a client ever again. After that experience, I found it best to not try to make any new friends for a while.

A little while after that incident, I got a phone call from Kalamazoo. It was Marla! She finally decided to give me a call and let me know that she had left Woody. She apologized for not believing me, and we both cried together over the phone. She also informed me that she would be moving to Chicago soon. I was happy for her and glad that we had finally made amends. Over the next few years, we wrote each other a few times a year, and we talked almost weekly. I was so happy to have my friend back.

*****

By the fall of 1963, my husband, my son, Joshua, who was now eight years old, and I moved from our little apartment off Woodward to a huge four-story apartment building on Chicago Boulevard in Detroit. We were both hired as managers and were able to obtain a nice unit on the second floor of the building.

The building was absolutely beautiful. The lobby was huge and had these large, gorgeous planters that flanked both sides of the entryway. Tufted leather benches sat along the walls to the left and to the right as you walked through the door to the stairs at the back of the lobby. A large, garnet-red wool carpet covered the center of the marble floor and led you right to, and up, the set of stairs. The lobby also had high, tall windows on either side that were accented with beautiful paisley drapes that hung from the ceiling to the floor.

This building's lobby was a sight for my eyes to behold. I was so excited to be living there. However, little did I know, things would change sooner than later.

One afternoon, I got a call from my older sister, Myrtle, asking if our younger sister, Doris, could come to Detroit and if I could help her find a place to stay. She was away at a teacher's college in New

York. She was about three months pregnant and did not want to continue school there while she was all alone and pregnant. I agreed with Myrtle that it would be best if Doris came to Detroit. Myrtle paid our brother, Carl Jr., to drive up to New York, pick up Doris, and bring her to me.

Thankfully, Joshua and I had just moved into the new apartment building, and since we were managers, I was able to get her an apartment right above ours. Doris and I went out almost every day, shopping and looking for furniture and household items at the resale and antique shops. We got her apartment all fixed up and furnished within three weeks. She was so happy to be living in the same building with me and Joshua. And quite honestly, I was just as happy.

In the spring of 1964, Doris gave birth to her beautiful baby girl. She named her Diane. That baby stole my heart immediately. She had the prettiest little round face and juicy little cheeks. Her eyes were soulful as if she had been here before. Joshua and I watched baby Diane during the day to allow Doris to continue in her education, which ultimately resulted in a teaching job. It all worked out so perfectly for everyone. Because we were able to continue managing the apartment building and taking care of the baby with no problem. And the months rolled on...

It was now the fall of 1965, and Joshua and I had been managing the building for about two years at this point. I was starting to go a little stir-crazy, living and working at the same place. I needed some excitement in my life.

Joshua and I loved each other dearly, but we started experiencing some issues because of our vast age difference. We weren't connecting physically as much as I would've liked, and this caused somewhat of a strain on our relationship. I was in my early thirties and he was in his sixties, and I wanted to be with him intimately a great deal more than he wanted. It wasn't that he didn't love me, it was just the big difference in our ages. I was in my prime while he was well past it.

One evening, Joshua and I had a long talk. He knew that I was becoming dissatisfied with things. He knew that I was missing my other family and Marla. Most of my siblings had moved to other states and were no longer living in Missouri. Doris was here, of course, and

Carl Jr. had also moved to Detroit, but he was always busy with his new wife and baby. Donald was living in Florida. Walter, Myrtle, and Judith were all living in Chicago. And Gregory was still locked up. I really missed everybody, so I asked Joshua if he would be open to moving to Chicago and explained to him why it would be good for us.

By this time, he was retired from the automotive corporation and was working part time as a security guard, so it wasn't like he would be leaving a whole lot behind. I tried for weeks to get him to consider it, but to no avail. He absolutely did not want to move. I was growing more and more restless. It was as if the city of Chicago was calling me and I needed to answer her. I wanted change, I needed change, and it seemed as though Chicago was the perfect place for it.

After a few more weeks and attempts to persuade Joshua, impressing upon him that our marriage needed a fresh start and letting him know that I was becoming unhappy, nothing changed. He had dug in his heels and had made it very clear to me that he wasn't going anywhere. So, it was then that I decided I would take Joshua Jr. and go to Chicago for a few weeks under the confines that it was just to visit for a while. My husband was apprehensive, but he gave me the go-ahead to visit with family for a few weeks. However, in my mind, I was going to see if there was a way that I could eventually make Chicago home.

# CHAPTER SIX

# Chicago, Here I Come

Joshua Jr. and I stepped off the train and was greeted by my sister, Myrtle, and her three children. She had two boys and one girl: DeAnna was six, Mark was eight, and Oliver was eleven. Oliver was the first of my siblings' children to be born. I always thought Oliver was a funny name, like something you'd name your puppy. But he was named after his father.

Myrtle got married to Oliver Sr. not long after she moved to Chicago. She met her husband through a lady that she was renting a place from. He was a very fair-skinned man with shiny, wavy hair. Although his name was Oliver, everyone called him by his initials, OD. Myrtle told me how he had a wonderful sense of humor and kept her laughing all the time. But what she didn't share with me right away was how he also had another side to him that wasn't so pleasant.

Through the hustle and bustle of the people exiting the train, Myrtle made her way over to me. We hugged as if we hadn't seen in each other in decades. I was so excited to be in Chicago and couldn't wait to spend time with my family! Our first stop was Myrtle's house, which is where Joshua Jr. and I would be staying. I needed to freshen up a bit, and then we would head over to see Judith. And I would be able to meet her new husband and baby girl.

I placed a call to my husband to let him know that Joshua Jr. and I made it safely to Chicago. Then Myrtle and I headed over to Judith's house. We spent a few hours at Judith's, laughing and talking about old times. I had really been missing my other sisters, and this was doing me a world of good just being in their presence. Our bond was so strong that it felt like we had not even been apart for the time that we had.

We talked about our childhood and how much we missed our mother and how much we disliked that mean ole Nellie. We talked about Daddy and how much he liked to cook and how good those cakes he'd bake used to smell. I started to get a little choked up when all those memories started flooding into my mind. But I didn't let my sisters see it. I kept it together long enough to use the excuse of having to go to the bathroom as a way to quickly leave the room.

When I returned, the conversation shifted to our children and husbands. My sisters had no idea that my husband and I were having any issues. Actually, if I was honest with myself, it would be better to say it was me who had the issues. Joshua was a good, wholesome, loving man. I really had no complaints in that area. My issue was more with the fact that he didn't like going out and that we didn't indulge in each other as often as I would've liked. But other than that, he was an awesome husband and father. Part of me felt guilty for leaving under false pretenses. But I figured that I needed this temporary break to see if it would need to be a permanent move or if I would return to Detroit after getting the desire to live in Chicago out of my system.

Judith clapped her hands really loud in my direction and yelled out, "Elizabeth!"

"Huh?"

"Girl, where was your mind at? I asked you a question, and you totally ignored me."

"I'm sorry, Judith. What did you say?"

With her hands on her hips, she playfully asked, "I said…how is it being married to an older man?"

"Oh, it's fine. The best part of it is that he lets me pretty much do whatever I want."

"Hahaha! I know that's right! If he knows what's good for him, he better! Because we all know that Elizabeth ain't nobody to play with!"

"No, I don't mean it like that. I'm just saying that because he's more laid back, he doesn't like to rip and run as much as I do, but he doesn't try to hold me back from doing it. If there is any place I want to go and he doesn't feel like going, he'll just say, 'Go ahead, baby. Have fun.' And I appreciate that about him."

Myrtle laughed and said, "Chile, I wish OD was that way. I can't seem to get away from his ass for nothing unless I'm at work."

We all laughed a little bit more and shared stories about married life well into the evening. It was getting late, so Myrtle and I decided to call it a night and let Judith get some rest.

When Myrtle and I got back to her house, OD greeted her at the door and asked her to step into their bedroom so they could talk. I could hear them arguing through the door, and then it was silent for quite a while. So, I decided to go get Oliver and Joshua from playing outside and made them get ready for bed, and I did the same.

The first few days there were somewhat uneventful. So that Saturday, we all decided to have a cookout over at Walter's place, my oldest brother. Me, my sisters, Judith and Myrtle, their husbands, and all the kids showed up ready to have a full day of family and fun. Walter and his wife had a swimming pool at the apartment building where they lived with their teenage daughter.

Walter had a buddy he called Bubba. Bubba came around often. But even more often when there was food being served. Walter and Bubba had to be over seven hundred pounds between the two of them. I hadn't seen Walter in years, and I was shocked at how big he had gotten. The two of them had an idea for some big invention, and they were excited about debuting it. And who better to debut it in front of other than family and friends?

We spent a great deal of the afternoon eating, playing bid whist, and listening to music out by the pool. After our food had digested, some of us decided to take a dip in the pool. Walter and Bubba perked up, and they both stood on the poolside to make their big announcement. Walter had come up with the concept, and Bubba was the one who created the final product. They both stood there beaming with pride as Walter explained how this invention came about.

"If I could have everyone's attention. My good friend, Bubba, and I have come up with a wonderful idea, and today is the first day we are going to try it out. You all are lucky to be able to behold this new invention that will hopefully make us very rich. The thought came to me one day while relaxing in the pool. What if my swimming shorts had the ability to allow me to float? This would be great for people who couldn't swim and would guarantee that they would not drown because the shorts would keep them at the surface of the water. So, my good ole buddy, Bubba, here was able to sew in several pieces of foam cushioning into the inside lining of a pair of shorts. These shorts are going to change the way we enjoy the water and hopefully save a few lives in the process. I'm going to go and change into the shorts, and when I return, be prepared to be amazed!"

We all hooted and cheered him on with great excitement. And when he returned, we all stood around the perimeter of the pool to behold the much-anticipated debut of Walter and Bubba's soon-to-be world-famous floatable swim shorts.

Walter approached the edge of the pool and started to rock backward and forward in an effort to give a dramatic dive into the deep end of the pool. He rocked one last time and launched himself into the water. A huge splash accompanied his plunge. We all cheered and clapped as he hit the water.

He went in face first, and that's exactly how he stayed in the water. Walter's floatable shorts did just what was intended, but for his rear end only. The foam cushions caused his rear end to stay above the water while his upper body remained submerged, and his entire head stayed under water.

We all howled with laughter, watching him struggle and splash around trying to bring his upper body up to the surface. After a few seconds of laughing, we all realized that he was going to drown if someone didn't help him. So, Bubba dove in, grabbed the waistband of his shorts, and pulled him safely to the pool's edge where he could grab hold and pull himself out. When he finally did, we all fell out laughing so hard at the two of them. It goes without saying that their invention never made it beyond the test phase.

We enjoyed each other's company well into the evening. So much so that I didn't want it to end. It was so refreshing to be around my family. I absolutely enjoyed every minute of it.

The next day, Myrtle and I got up early and made breakfast for the kids and OD. Then she and I went downtown, with her daughter DeAnna in tow, to do a little sightseeing, browsing through a few shops, with a final stop at the Buckingham Fountain just along Lake Shore Drive and Lake Michigan. It was an absolutely lovely day for us girls.

Myrtle, in particular, did not want it to end because she had to go to work the next day. She had a very good job working at a major manufacturing company that made cookies and snacks. She loved her job, but I know that since I was there visiting, she would have liked to be able to stay home an extra day or two so that we could spend more time together. As the midday sun started its decline and the water of Lake Michigan glistened with an amber glow, we decided it was time to call it a day and head back home.

Monday, while Myrtle was at work and the kids were with OD, I decided to go pay Marla a visit. She had been in Chicago for a while now. She lived in a four-family flat on the south side of town, which was not too far from where Myrtle was staying. So, I caught the "L" train to her place. The "L" is Chicago's aboveground mass transit system. This was exciting! I was going to ride the "L" for the first time in my life, and I knew it would not disappoint. While taking a ride on the "L," I saw my share of sights, and I ain't talking about the buildings and landmarks. I'm talking about the people. The people in Chicago were lively and much more animated than folks in Detroit. To me, Detroit was a much slower paced place to live.

When I arrived at Marla's door, I was filled with a nervous excitement. I was so anxious to see her. By this time, Marla had a second daughter. The oldest daughter looked just like her father, Woody, like that fool spit her out. The youngest looked just like Marla. One of Marla's cousins was staying with her in Chicago so she would watch the girls while Marla worked.

When Marla opened the door, we both let out a scream, grabbed each other, and rocked back and forth really fast while we hugged. I could smell her famous peach cobbler from the front stoop.

I loosened my grip, stood back, and said with excitement, "Girl, is the aroma coming from in there what I think it is?"

"I don't know what you're talking about. I ain't got nothing in here for you but love, baby!"

"Marla, don't play with me. You know I smell that peach cobbler. And I want me a big ole heap of it in a bowl with some vanilla ice cream on top. You know how we used to do!"

"Hahaha! Don't I know it! Come on in, girl. I made this one just for you!"

We took our seats at her little kitchenette table, and when she opened that oven door, I thought I was going to lose my mind. The aroma from that cobbler had my mouth watering so tough and sent my stomach instantly into growling. I couldn't wait to sink my teeth into it. She pulled out a white porcelain bowl from the cupboard and spooned out a nice big heap of that hot, steamy peach cobbler and heaped it right into my bowl. The crust was perfectly golden brown, and it was just the right ratio of peaches to juice to crust. Before I could remove my gaze from this glorious sight, she added two large scoops of vanilla ice cream right on top of the mound of cobbler. The ice cream began to slowly melt, forming small white streams of creamy goodness down every side of the cobbler, which started to pool into a small moat of melted ice cream around the base of the cobbler.

When I took my first bite, I'm sure my eyes rolled to the back of my head. I had died and gone to heaven. I savored every single bite of that cobbler and ice cream. I've always had a healthy appreciation for really good soul food. It's like nothing else! I especially can appreciate a person who could throw down in the kitchen. And Marla was one of those people—she could definitely throw down.

Marla and I got caught up so good that it was as if we didn't miss a beat. She told me all about her past dealings with her ex, Woody, and I caught her up to speed on what was going on in my life. We laughed and cried. We missed each other so much, and it was good to have my old friend back again.

Marla really did have a good heart. She was a giving person, almost to fault. She told me how she let some man borrow some money from her, and he had been dodging her for the past two weeks.

"Girl, listen here. I'm an expert at collecting what's owed to me. I got a little time on my hands today if you wanna try and find this jackass and get your money back."

With an excited smile on her face, Marla replied, "Chile, yes! Let me get my car keys and shoes."

She left the kitchen for a few seconds and reappeared with her keys in hand and shoes on her feet. She was ready to roll. We started out at the place where the man worked. He wasn't there. One of his coworkers said that he left early that day and that he would likely be at the local bar on Ninety-Fifth Street. So, that's where we were headed next.

As we pulled up to the bar, I asked her if she knew what kind of car he drove. She said yes and was able to point it out to me in the parking area next to the bar. I told her that I thought it would be best to wait outside and allow him to walk toward his car, and that's when we would get out of Marla's car and meet him right at his vehicle before he would be able to get in. So, we waited and waited. We waited so long that we lost focus for a moment and allowed him to slip past us.

Our attention was quickly refocused when we heard a car door close, and to our surprise, it was him about to drive off. We decided to follow him. We trailed behind him as he drove to his next destination. When he got to where he was going and parked, we quickly jumped out of our vehicle and confronted him. I had my purse strapped to me with my revolver and my dagger inside. And depending on how foolish he wanted to be would determine which one I would need to pull out. Marla didn't have a weapon. All she had was somewhat of a self-satisfied smirk on her face.

"Hey, hey! Yoo-hoo! I know you didn't think you were gonna get away with not paying me my money back, did you?"

He did a 180-degree swivel on the heels of his ole ugly Florsheim brown ankle boots, and when he caught sight of Marla, he stepped back on his right leg and folded his arms with an arrogant grin and condescending stare. He looked me and Marla up and down as if he had absolutely no concern for whatever we had planned.

"I know you don't think you can just run up on me and expect me to shake in my boots and just hand you over some money, do you? I would suggest that you and your friend get back in your car and drive your asses on away from here."

Marla started cursing and flailing her arms all around while issuing out threats about what she would do to him if he didn't pay up. And his response was to simply laugh, shake his head, and wave his hand at her as if he was swatting at a fly. I politely interrupted Marla by putting my hand on her shoulder and telling her to calm down.

I said in a calm voice but loud enough for him to hear, "That's okay, Marla. I bet I got something that will make him come off that money in two seconds flat!"

I reached into my purse and pulled out my pistol, being sure to conceal it in such a way that it wouldn't be too obvious that I was pointing it dead at him. But I made sure that he could see it. And when he did see it, his eyes got big as saucers. He flung up his hands and started stammering.

"Hey, hey, hey. Hold on! Hold it, nah! I don't want no trouble. It ain't that serious. I got your money right here."

He slowly reached to pull up the cuff of his pants to expose his sock and the top edge of his boot. "I got some money right here in my sock."

My heart started to pound because I wasn't sure if money was all he had hidden in them ugly-ass boots. I had my trigger finger lightly on the trigger of my pistol, so if he tried to pull anything other than money out that boot, I was ready for him. He maintained eye contact with me and saw that I looked nervous. He offered reassurance.

"Hey, nah, I'm just reaching for the money. Don't shoot. I ain't got nothing in here but money."

He slowly pulled out a small stack of bills folded in half. He unfolded the money and pulled out what he owed her and tossed it on the grass at her feet.

"She ain't no dog! Pick it up and hand it to her like you got some sense!"

He apologized and walked slowly toward her with his left hand in the air while reaching down for the money with his other hand. He picked up the money and handed it to her. Marla snatched it from his hand.

"Yeah…gimme my money! And maybe next time you'll think twice before you try and pull something like this on somebody else. With yo nickel-slick talking, cheap-suit-wearing broke ass!"

As I continued to point the gun in his direction, Marla and I hopped back into her car and drove away. And as we drove away, we both fell out laughing. We were so tickled about how big and bad he thought he was until he got a gander at the piece I was carrying.

I loved spending time with Marla again. It was so much fun, and we always seemed to have an adventurous or exciting time whenever we got together. I hated that I had to soon leave and go back to Detroit.

I spent another week in Chicago, but I knew I had to head back to my home and husband in Detroit. I wish I could bottle up the fun and adventure of Chicago and take it all back with me. But while there, I did come to realize that I sort of took my husband for granted. He was an excellent father and a loving husband. I needed to cool my heels and return home with my son and try to focus on what was good in my marriage.

*****

Realizing that I have been talking for quite some time, I pause to acknowledge the fact that Aurora is probably getting tired of sitting at my bedside in this hospital and likely ready to go. The sun is rising, and it's probably the end of her shift.

"My Lord, I know you must be tired. You have been sitting there listening to me ramble on and on. I'm sure I've been talking for at least a couple of hours now. Wouldn't you like to go and get yourself some rest?"

"Well, Elizabeth, your story is captivating. It makes me want to hear even more about you. These past several days have been very enjoyable."

Surprised that she mentioned it being several days, I interrupt her. "Wait. What? Did you say several days?"

Aurora replies with a bit of consolation in her voice. "Yes, it's been four days now. I know it seems like it's only been one night, but when you're in a twilight state, it can seem that way. Your children have even stopped by to visit you."

"When was this? I don't recall ever being interrupted while I've been talking. And I certainly don't remember two additional days passing."

I guess she can sense the anxiety in my voice, so she quickly diverts the conversation. "Your sons and daughter should be coming in to visit with you shortly. So, I should be leaving now. But don't worry, I'll be back tonight, and we can pick up where you left off. I'll see you then, Elizabeth."

And the instant she leaves, I feel groggy and have another splitting headache. I hear the door to my room open and close, and I suddenly hear my children talking, but I can't see them or respond to them. My heart is racing because I'm now feeling just like I did when I first got here but worse. My daughter, Sheryl, is called out the room and returns in a matter of minutes.

She's whimpering, and I can hear the distress in her voice.

"They want to move her tomorrow. I just went ahead and chose a place in Redford Township over by the house. That way we can continue to visit her every day without having to travel so far. I just wish she would wake up."

All the while Joshua Jr. and Darryl are consoling her, I'm trying my best to say something to them. I want to tell them everything will be okay. But I can't. At this point, I can't even reassure myself of that. All I can do at this point is wait and see what the end will be.

As I hear my children talking among themselves, another person enters the room. It's a lady's voice.

"How's she doing today?"

Darryl and Joshua Jr. both speak simultaneously. "Not much change."

Joshua continues, "We can't seem to get her to wake up."

Then the lady says, "Yeah, well, she's heavily medicated. We're just trying to keep her comfortable, particularly since she's about to be transported. We don't want her to be in any pain. So, I'm here to administer her pain meds now."

Sheryl asks, "How much longer do you think she has?"

The lady responds, "It's hard to tell. Let's just take it day by day. Just keep visiting with her. I like to believe that when patients are in this state, they can still hear what's going on around them."

Now I'm really confused. What does she mean when she says in this state? Maybe she's referring to the fact that they have me on so much medication that I can barely keep up with what's going on. One minute I'm in pain and unable to speak, the next minute I feel totally fine, and now I'm right back at square one. And it appears the only time I can respond to anyone is when Aurora, my patient sitter, is here alone with me.

This is crazy! I can't take it…I want to scream! I want to sit up and let everyone know that I can hear them discussing me. I want to be able to communicate with my children. I want to go home!

Some time has passed, and I can now open my eyes and see that I'm alone again. Once more, it's dark, and my room is silent. But I'm in a different room. Although it's dark, I can tell that this room is decorated more nicely and has a homey feel to it. I hear a shuffling noise near the entrance of the room, and I try to focus.

I feel a warm sensation, and now there's a soft, warm glow at the foot of my bed. I'm squinting to try to focus more clearly. And I can make out a figure coming closer to me in the midst of the glow. As it gets closer, I see it's Aurora. The glow must've been the light from the hallway as she entered the room. In any case, I must admit that I'm a little relieved to see her.

But what is she doing here? Am I in the same hospital but just in a different room? I thought my daughter said that they were transporting me to a different location near our house? And if so, how is it that Aurora is here with me?

"Hello, Elizabeth. I see they have you all set up here at the Redford Healthcare Facility."

And just as I suspected, I'm able to speak again with no discomfort. "Hi, Aurora. Yeah, I guess so. But what are you doing here too?"

"I go wherever my assignment takes me. Wherever you go, I go."

"Okay. So, you must not work directly for the hospital. You work for some sort of agency that's contracted to serve people no matter what medical facility they're in?"

"Yes, sort of like that. Basically, I provide service to whomever, wherever it's needed, as commissioned by the one who has charge over me."

I know she could tell I was still not all the way clear on how she's able to follow me from one place to another, and who the heck is "the one who has charge over" her? Well, whatever, she's a welcome breath of fresh air, and she obviously came with a fresh pair of ears ready to listen again.

# *Detroit, Here I Come (Again...)*

It had been a few months since I got back from Illinois. I finally shook my intense desire to live in Chicago. What I realized since returning home is that I actually preferred the slower pace of things in Detroit. Chicago was fun and all, but the people appeared to be so hurried and less congenial than the folks in Detroit. I didn't really have a desire to be a part of the nightclub scene, and the excitement from all the sightseeing had long run its course. I had a life here in Detroit with my husband, son, sister, niece, etc. So, it was time for me to put my focus back on the people and things that mattered.

It was an added bonus that just about a month after I had returned home, Marla called me and told me that she had decided that she missed our fun times together so much that she planned to pick up everything and moved to Detroit too. She arrived in Detroit a few months after that. She sought out a family member in Detroit who helped her find a job working as a seamstress in a local cleaners. She also had plans to move into a small apartment for herself and her two girls.

It was just like old times. We spent a great deal of our time together on the weekends, playing cards, shopping, and such. She had always been someone I could be myself with and confide in, and I knew it would not go beyond her. I told her about the span of time where I was experiencing some challenges in my marriage, and she never told anyone. She was loyal like that. I loved her like a sister.

As time went on, my life finally became more settled. At least as far as someone on the outside looking in. As far as family and friends were concerned, all appeared fine, but honestly, I was still having moments within my marriage where I felt a little unfulfilled. I had even battled with thoughts of giving in to certain temptations. I had been faced with an opportunity to secretly stray, but I didn't want to further complicate an already complex emotional ride I found myself on.

It was now a couple of days after the New Year, and I was looking for 1967 to be a more resolved one for me and my bundle of emotions. I had done my share of celebrating and bringing in the New Year at an after-hours joint with family and friends, and I was hoping that it wasn't something I ate because I was not feeling my best. I had several days of illness that led me to make an appointment with a doctor at a hospital a few miles away in Highland Park, Michigan. Well, needless to say, I found out that it wasn't food poisoning. I was pregnant again.

I was excited to know that I would be having another child. But I'd be lying if I said that I wasn't also a bit nervous. I had all sorts of emotions swirling around in me. I knew that I wanted to expand my family, but I just wasn't sure if this was the right time. But as the saying goes, time waits for no one. And in what seemed like a flash, it was July, and I was expecting to deliver in mid-August.

On July 23, I awoke to the radio being played loudly. My husband, Joshua, often got up early and would sit and listen to the radio while drinking his morning cup of coffee. But what I couldn't understand was why he had the volume up so loud! I quickly got up, threw on my housecoat, and made my way to the kitchen where I knew he would be. He was sitting there with a concerning fixed look on his face and his head leaned in close as if the news announcer guy was talking right into his ear.

When I entered the kitchen, I was ready to fuss at him about having the darn thing up so loud, but he held up his hand to silence me before I could even get a word out. He then put his finger to his lips to ensure my silence. "Shh...wait."

I took a seat at the opposite end of the table and leaned in to listen too. The announcer was describing some sort of disturbance after a raid that took place within just a few miles of our apartment on Twelfth Street. I just shook my head and started pouring myself a glass of cold water.

Unfortunately, it wasn't the first time I had heard of the police raiding one of our neighborhood spots. They were always driving around looking for some black folks to harass. Joshua stayed glued to that radio for the next several hours as if he was almost anticipating something more to come of the incident. And sure enough, later that evening, the city of Detroit had a full-fledged riot on its hands. And by 8:00 p.m. that evening, the city's mayor had enacted a citywide curfew that started at about 9:00 p.m. that night.

By this time, we were now in front of the television set, and the news of the riot had spread, along with several other uprisings throughout the city. It was so bad that the National Guard had to be called in. We stayed in our apartment that night and well into the following evening. By that Tuesday, it had gotten so bad that the president had to call in federal troops. And by Wednesday, there were actual tanks rolling down my street!

I couldn't believe it. I was so afraid. Here I was, good and pregnant, nine months to be exact, and I was held up in my apartment with my family, not knowing if our building would be one that the rioters would decide to target. I only had a couple of weeks to go before my anticipated delivery. and I was scared. Thankfully, by that Thursday or Friday, some level of order was restored, but the death and destruction left behind was something that our poor city never really bounced back from.

Just seventeen days after the riots ended, I gave birth to another beautiful baby boy. We named him Darryl. He was a very fair-complexioned baby with a head full of curly brown hair and a pronounced nose. I thought he was simply adorable.

There was a particular nurse at the hospital that would stare at my baby every time she came into the room. She was a white lady who looked to be in her midfifties. I have to admit it kind of made me mad that she was so fixated on my baby. I couldn't figure out what her issue was. So, I just came out and asked her.

"Is there something the matter?"

"Oh no, honey. I was just admiring how nice-looking your baby is." She paused and leaned in to take a closer peek at him. "He's a little yellow fella, isn't he? He looks just like a little Jew baby."

I flinched and adjusted his swaddling blanket to protect him slightly from her gaze.

"Oh, honey, I didn't mean anything by it. I was just saying he looks a little fair. He looks like…"

I cut her off, "He looks like me and his father. And we ain't Jewish!"

She quickly switched her focus from the baby to me. She gave me a sharp glance then swiftly turned and walked out the room. It's amazing to me how some people have so much nerve. Later that day, I had a couple more hospital staff members come to my room to check in on us. But I knew that they were there to be nosy. The doctor even gave his two cents on my baby's complexion and features.

I didn't care what those white nurses and doctors had to say. He may have been fair, and after looking at his features, I myself even had to admit that he looked like he was a from a Jewish family, but he was mine. I could tell by looking at the shade of his skin on the outer rim of his ears that his skin would certainly darken up a little later. But none of that really mattered. He was my baby and a wonderful birthday gift from God to me. He was born just two days before my birthday. I was so happy to have another wonderful addition to my life and family. I stayed in the hospital a few more days and was eventually released to go home with my new baby boy.

Things were quiet on the streets after the riot. Business owners and the community were cleaning up and trying to figure out what was next. Much of the area where we lived looked like a war zone. There were burned-out businesses and vandalized buildings everywhere! It hurt my heart so much to see Detroit in this state. I couldn't believe the level of devastation that it was left in. After the '67 riots, Detroit was never the same. Thankfully, our apartment building survived it all.

That following year, things started to feel like they were going back to normal. My youngest sister, Doris, had met a man who worked for one of the automotive companies and got married not long after they started dating. Her husband moved in with her, and I was able to get a bigger apartment for them on another floor in our building.

Doris and I held quite a few card parties and invited friends over to play darn near every weekend. Those were great times! We would stay up well past midnight, slamming cards on the table with a generous amount of arrogance when a book was earned or if a game was won. There was good music, good food, good friends, and a hell of a lot of good fun!

Aside from the weekly card parties, there was always something going on in the building that would warrant conversation while it was my turn to deal the cards. I would tell my friends about all the goings-on that took place the week prior. This was a jovial source of entertainment. They loved it when I told my stories.

I remember one time a man in our apartment building was late with his rent. So, I put a note on his door to remind him that we needed him to pay his back rent or face eviction the next month. He obviously didn't like that I had done that, so he stopped by our apartment to let us know.

At the time, Doris's husband, Eugene, was there with us, spending a little time before he had to go to work, to sit and talk with Joshua about their favorite subjects—politics and current events. There was a loud, hard knock at our door, so I had my husband go check it out.

"Who is it?"

The response came with some obvious agitation in the voice, "Man, it's Jasper from two floors up! I need to speak to y'all right now!"

Joshua opened the door, and Mr. Jasper started in on him, cursing and pointing his finger in his face. I immediately hopped up and went to go put the baby in his crib. While I was in there, I could hear them going back and forth and my sister's husband telling them to both calm down. Then I heard what sounded like furniture moving and Eugene yelling for me.

"Elizabeth, come here quick! Call the police on this fool!"

I knew what I had to do, and it wasn't calling no police. As I returned from the back bedroom, I saw that Mr. Jasper and my husband had each other in a dual locked embrace, like two pro wrestlers, and Eugene wasn't doing anything but dancing around them like a referee and chuckling the whole time.

"Turn him loose!" I yelled.

But Mr. Jasper wasn't responding to my plea. So, I hit him on his back with what was in my hand to get his attention. He swung around with rage in his face, but when his eyes registered what I was holding in my hand, his expression changed.

He looked at me and immediately put up his hands. "What the hell? Wait, wait, wait, please!"

"Oh, yeah, you begging now, huh? Just a minute ago you came here like you were all big and bad! You're in here tearing up my place all because you can't handle your own business! You should've just paid what you owe! But now you here fighting with my husband and disturbing my home! Get yo lowlife'd tail up outa here before I put a plug in your ass!"

I pointed and pressed my gun right directly in the middle of his chest and backed his ignorant tail out through my apartment door and into the hallway. Our apartment was right next to the stairwell, so I walked him backward in that direction. Once I got him to the door of the stairwell, my husband had caught up with us, and Eugene was hanging his head out of our apartment door, laughing.

Mr. Jasper did a slow 180-degree turn toward the stairs, with his hands still in the air. And as he was getting ready to make his descent, I raised my right foot and kicked him square in the crack of his behind. He sailed down those stairs like a bat out of hell! He was running like the wind was carrying him.

He yelled, "You crazy as hell!"

"Yeah, crazy as they come! Now, make sure you have that rent money by the end of this week!"

When I turned around from watching him fly down the stairs, I saw Eugene and Joshua slapping each other's backs, breathing hard, laughing, and shaking their heads in disbelief. I was fired up with adrenaline and anger, but when I saw them laughing, I burst out into laughter right along with them. That would turn into another story to share over our next Saturday night card game.

There was always something going on in that building. And Lord knows I found myself in the middle of a lot of action that went on there simply because Joshua and I were managers. If it wasn't someone trying to skip on paying their rent, it was someone stealing items and fixtures from the grand lobby.

One day in particular, it was a lot of commotion coming from the hallway. There was a young couple who lived in the apartment two doors down from ours. The young lady was a sweetheart. She worked at a doctor's office as a receptionist and was also going to school to become a nurse. Her boyfriend was supposedly an auto mechanic, but I never actually saw him go to work. All I ever saw him do was sit out on the front stoop of the building and drink and wait for her to come home with some money or groceries.

He was also a stone-cold alcoholic, and he would often jump on her whenever he got ready. I never heard them, but I would often see the bruises and black eyes that she would try to hide. But this time, I could hear them fighting out in the hallway, and I wasn't going to ignore it. I went to my door, opened it up, and took a look at what was going on.

This guy was beating that poor girl right there in the middle of the hallway. Joshua wasn't home, and I had just finished putting Darryl down for a nap. I yelled out for him to stop, but he just kept right on hitting and yelling at her. I wasn't about to stand there and let him use her as a punching bag, so once again I had to do something to get him off her. She fell to the floor, balled herself up in the fetal position, and he started kicking her. I went to my bedroom to grab what I needed to put an end to this. Then I marched out my apartment door and right over to them.

With a strange sense of calmness in my voice, I said, "If you hit or kick her one more time, it's gonna be your last time."

"Mind your business before I beat your ass like I'm beating hers!"

I slowly raised my hand from my side and pointed my gun toward his head. "I'd like to see you try. I'll drop you right where you stand. I ain't afraid to go to jail. And I'll gladly go today, if that's what you want."

I could see her out the corner of my eye, shivering and crying on the floor. I kept my gaze on him while motioning for her to get up.

"C'mon, get up, sweetie. He might be crazy, but he ain't stupid. He's not gon' hurt you no more, I guarantee you that!"

Then I announced to him that this was his last day in my building. I had her go to my apartment to clean herself up while I walked him to her apartment door. I told him he had fifteen minutes to grab whatever he could and shove it in a suitcase because that day would be his last day living there. And as far as I know, that was the last time she saw him.

I had a reputation in that building. Well, pretty much among anyone who knew me. I didn't take no mess from nobody. Not anyone…and especially not from a no-good man. I have never had a tolerance for that. I couldn't see myself getting up and going to work every day while the man I'm with is lying up in the bed every day with his toes pointed toward heaven. I don't care if he had to get out there in the streets to collect and crush glass bottles to sell for recycling! He better hustle and do something to contribute to the household.

As for the young lady that I helped in the hallway that day, a year later, she caught me coming in from the grocery store and handed me an invitation to her graduation from nursing school. She thanked me and gave me the biggest hug that warmed my soul. I was so happy to see that she had stayed free of that guy and accomplished her goal of becoming a nurse. She eventually moved out and carried on with her life, but I was privileged and happy to know that she would do just fine for herself.

And there was more good news to come. Myrtle called from Chicago and asked Doris and me to meet her in St. Louis to go to a hearing regarding our brother, Gregory, who was still in prison. I wasn't able to go because I was still nursing. And even though Doris was pregnant again, she caught the train down to St. Louis, where she and Myrtle had an opportunity to speak with the warden of the prison immediately following the hearing.

The warden was a middle-aged white man who, according to them, was enamored with their beauty. So much so that he requested that they indulge him and agree to spend some additional time there with him, chatting over lunch in his office. After an hour or more of conversation and mild flirtation, they told me that the warden promised them that our brother would be released within the week. And so it was, our brother, Gregory, was released from a life sentence for murder. Myrtle and Doris believed it was all because the warden liked the way they looked and carried themselves.

But I really believe it was all by the grace of God that it went down that way. Soon after his release, Gregory moved to Chicago to be near our other siblings so he could get the support he needed there with them. The month after Gregory's release and Doris returned home, she gave birth to her second child, a boy. I was so excited because her son and my youngest son would be able to play and grow together.

A couple more years rolled by, and the majority of my siblings seemed to be doing pretty well. However, my oldest brother, Walter, had just sent word through a phone call that he and his wife's beautiful one and only daughter had passed away. My niece was a stunningly beautiful girl. She had passed away in her sleep. She was in her early twenties and had two small children of her own, so we all knew that this was going to be hard on the family. I knew I had to make my way to Chicago to be a support to my brother and his family. By the weekend, we all had made plans to head to Chicago for the funeral.

Coincidently, while we were all preparing to get on the road from our various locations, we got word that Myrtle's mother-in-law had passed away also. So, both funerals were on the same weekend. Once in town, I stayed with Myrtle and OD while Doris stayed with our bonus sister, Judith. Our next oldest brother, Carl Jr., stayed with a friend of his in Chicago. And our youngest brother, Donald, flew up from Florida and stayed with Walter and his wife. Although the circumstances surrounding our coming together was indeed sad, it was nice to have the Davidson clan back together again. Even Walter was excited to see all his younger siblings together again. I don't think we've all been in the same town at the same time since we were kids.

My niece's funeral was that Friday, and OD's mother's funeral was the next day. While I was in the washroom at Myrtle's house, getting ready to head out to services for our niece, I heard the phone ring a couple of times, then a long pause, and about a minute or two later, it rang again. When I exited the washroom, I assumed it was my husband, Joshua, calling to make sure I made it okay. He stayed home with the boys.

I asked Myrtle, "Was that Joshua calling? I forgot to call him when I got here to let him know that I made it safely."

"Oh, no. It was a wrong number."

"Oh, okay. Well, let me see your phone. I should probably call him before we set out to go to the funeral."

Just as she was handing me the phone, it rang again, so I picked up the receiver, and before I could say anything, I heard a woman's screechy voice yell out "Bitch!" and then she slammed the phone down.

My mouth fell open, and I laughed. "Girl, some woman just called here. And all she said was 'Bitch' and hung up the phone. Ha ha, what in the world?"

As I looked at Myrtle, I saw that I was the only one who found it humorous.

"What? You must know this heifer or something."

She took a big breath and explained. "I wanted to wait until later to share this with you, but oh well. Yes, I know exactly who that is. Her name is Claudine, and she lives down on the next block. I found out that she and OD were having an affair for about a year. He and I have been on shaky ground for a while, and I'm really not sure if I want to work things out. I just want to get past his mother's funeral, and then we'll have to see. But she keeps calling here to harass me. I guess she figures if she keeps harassing me that I'll get into it with OD and leave him for sure, and he'll go running into her arms. I don't know!"

My heart started racing. I wanted to see this Claudine lady. "Which house does she live in because we can just go pay her a visit before we go to this funeral, and I guarantee you she won't be calling your phone no more. Now I guarantee you that!"

Myrtle chuckled a little bit. Probably because she remembered how I was when we were kids and how I used to take up for all of them and fight off the bullies.

"No, no. Elizabeth, I don't think that will be necessary. OD says that he cut things off with her and that he would handle her calling here. But I don't care what he does. Hell, she can have him if that's what she wants. I'm about done with him and his foolishness anyway."

"Yeah, well, if she doesn't leave you alone, I'll handle it myself!"

We left out and met the rest of our siblings at the funeral home. The service for my niece was beautiful yet somber. It was difficult to comprehend how such a wonderful young woman could be taken and leave behind a young husband and her two small children. She was a good person, mother, wife, and daughter. I know my brother and sister-in-law were both hurt, and there was nothing anyone could do to take away or even numb the pain. No one ever thinks that they'll have to bury their child. That's probably the biggest fear of any parent—to see your child pass on before you.

After the funeral, we all met over at Judith's house and took the time together as an opportunity to love on each other and catch up. We didn't linger too long into the evening because we all knew that we would have to get up early the next morning and do it all over again at the funeral of OD's mother.

It was an unusually cold fall morning. Although the sun was shining bright that day, it deceived all who dared to emerge from their homes to be greeted by the bitterly cold brisk wind. At about 8:00 a.m., the phone rang. OD was in the shower, and Myrtle was getting herself and the kids ready, so I answered the phone.

"Hello?"

The caller on the other end responded with a loud "Bitch!"

I felt my temperature rise. After the funeral was over, I planned on making Myrtle show me where this woman lived. I was going to show her what a bitch looks like. When Myrtle came downstairs to the kitchen where I was, she saw me hanging up the phone on the wall. I must've had a look on my face that clued her in on who it was that called.

"Was it her again?"

"Yes, and we're paying her a visit later today."

Myrtle sighed and wiped her brow. "Oh, Lord."

She was so busy rushing to get the kids and herself ready that she didn't have time to give much feedback on what she had already planned. I found out later that Myrtle had already set in her mind that if that woman showed up to the funeral, then she was going to deal with her personally.

We all arrived at the church where the services were being held. The service was nice and to the point. Afterward, some of us were standing in the foyer while others were in the sanctuary talking. OD was outside and had gone to get the car.

And lo and behold, that heifer came walking up the middle aisle, hugging and greeting members of OD's family as if she was a celebrity. As Claudine was going about greeting folks, she was gradually getting closer to Myrtle. I was unaware of all this at the time. So, before I knew anything, Myrtle grabbed Claudine by the collar. She got right in her face.

"Come here. I wanna talk to you! You the bitch that's been calling my house and cursing me out!"

Myrtle was pulling and tugging on Claudine with such force that it looked like she was getting ready to sling her to the floor. At that time, a couple of ministers at the church were walking by and caught sight of what was going on.

One spoke up and said, "Y'all ought to be ashamed of yourselves. You're in the house of the Lord."

Myrtle replied, "I don't care about this being a church. This tramp has been asking for me to beat her ass, and if the house of the Lord is where it needs to happen, then so be it!"

By that time, I caught up to Myrtle. "Myrtle, what's going on?"

"This is that bitch that's been calling me every day for a whole year."

My heart started racing as if it was pumping and priming itself to prepare me for war. "Let's get her!" I yelled.

By this time, Claudine made her escape out the foyer, out the front door, and down the stairs to the street. But we kept up with her. Once on the street in front of the church, I caught up to Claudine and grabbed her by the collar with my left hand and was winding up my right fist, like Popeye the Sailorman, to land a marvelous blow to her face. But I was barely able to get a hit in when my brother, Gregory, grabbed my right arm and stopped me.

"Elizabeth, no! You-you-you're g-g-g-gon' kill her!"

I snatched my arm away from him and yelled back, "As long as you're black, don't you ever grab me while I'm fighting!"

Meanwhile, all my siblings, along with a few others, had crowded around. I saw Doris standing near the curb, her fur stole draped across her shoulders, with a wonderfully amused grin on her face as she bore witness to the goings-on. And if the commotion got too close to her, she'd take a dainty step or two out of the way, all while enjoying the spectacle. At the same time, Judith got down on her hands and knees and crawled between somebody's legs so she could get her a few good licks in on Claudine too.

During the brawl, Claudine's hat was knocked off, and Myrtle's oldest son, Oliver Jr., picked it up and asked whose it was. Somebody said it was Claudine's hat, so he threw it back down, and it got trampled in the thick of things. By this time, OD was back with the car and had parked down the street. And the next thing we knew, he scooped up Myrtle and ran with her in his arms, like a roadrunner, back toward the car.

By then, some folks from the church came and eventually defused the situation. But I yelled out to Claudine, "If you call my sister again, I'm personally coming to pay you a visit!"

A couple of hours after that, we were all over at Myrtle's house hanging out. While everybody was getting comfortable and settled down, I got hold of OD, pulled him into a corner of the room, and laid into him something fierce. I read him up and down and warned him not to ever put my sister in a situation like that again.

He had no rebuttal. He just said, "Okay, Elizabeth. I got it, I got it."

After I was sure he got my point, I relieved him from my rant and went back over to where my brothers and sisters were gathered. Myrtle's house wasn't that big, so it was a little tight, but we didn't mind. We were just happy to be together. Some of us were on the couch, some at the dining room table, and some were even sitting on the floor.

OD made his way out to the garage to take some time to consider what I had told him, I guess. But the rest of us were just sitting around, laughing and recalling the events from earlier, when the phone rang, and Myrtle answered it. It was Claudine again, telling Myrtle to meet her outside.

When Myrtle hung up, she told us who it was and what she said. So, we all started scrambling through the pile of shoes at the door, trying to hurry up to go meet this heifer outside.

Across the street, there was some construction work going on, and little did we know that at that precise time, the crew was getting ready to set off some explosives to collapse part of the structure. So, right when we were getting our shoes on, we heard a loud KABOOM!

Someone yelled out, "Hit the lights!"

Somebody did hit the lights, and we all simultaneously hit the floor! Hahaha! We thought we were all so big and bad, but when we heard what we thought might've been a shotgun, we were truly scared!

Then Myrtle screamed, "Oh my god! OD is outside!"

So, my brothers went outside to check on him. When they came back in, they were all laughing because they knew by this time what that loud boom actually was. They told us, and we all just fell out laughing and clowning each other on how fast we each hit the floor. After all that excitement, we never did make it down the street to meet Claudine. Who knows, she was probably just as shaken as we were by the explosion, or maybe she thought we did it!

The next morning, I got back on the road to go home.

I was excited to return to Detroit because a few days prior to me going to Chicago, my husband and I decided it was time to get out of apartment management and start considering other options for employment so that we could eventually buy ourselves a home. Our thought behind that was mostly because it was becoming more and more difficult to deal with all the drama that managing that building brought with it. And trying to raise two boys in the process was starting to become very stressful. So, it was time for a change.

Thankfully, Joshua was able to go back to doing security at a local company, and I had an interview with the post office lined up. I eventually got the job with the post office but soon realized that mail delivery wasn't for me. I was later blessed with a job working for the state unemployment office.

I had been working there about a year when we found a home on the northwest side of Detroit. It was a beautiful, red brick, colonial style home with three bedrooms. My sister Doris had also just purchased a huge home in a historical neighborhood of the city. More good news soon followed.

Marla announced to me that she got engaged to a guy named Wilson Crafton she met at her new job with an automotive manufacturing company. She had been working there for a few months before they met. Less than a year later, they were married, and she, too, purchased a home with her new husband within a mile and a half from where I had just moved. It was something special that we all had found our new homes around the same time.

It was a few months later when I discovered that I was pregnant again. And this time, it was a girl. My baby girl Sheryl was born in the spring of 1972. I was so full of joy and loved being a mother. My children were the world to me. I was fortunate to be able to take several months of maternity leave from work after Sheryl was born and enjoyed spending time at home raising my children.

Much of my time was spent taking care of my kids, cooking and sewing. I taught myself how to sew, and I was so proud of an outfit that I made for myself. It was an all-white, short-sleeved leisure suit with a bright multicolor sleeveless top to wear underneath the jacket. It was made of a durable blend of polyester. It was casual, so I'd wear it out when I had to take care of business or run errands.

I remember one day I wore it out to go to the bank and to the grocery store. I wanted to pick up a few items to cook for dinner. I was in sort of a rush that day, so I handed off the baby to my husband, slapped on my wig, sprayed on a little perfume, grabbed my purse, and headed out of the door.

The bank was my first stop. After handling my business there, I stopped at the grocery store that I usually go to, which was close to my house. I wanted to make a nice dinner for my husband and the boys tonight. It had been a while since I cooked because, thankfully, Joshua liked to cook and bake, and he was good at it. He reminded me of my father in that respect.

I pulled into the grocery store parking lot and started to make my way toward the front entrance. As I was walking, I heard a loud buzz in my ear. I swatted away what I thought might've been a fly. There it was again but louder… "Buzz!" I swatted it away again, but this time I got a glimpse of it and realized it was not a fly but a big ole black-and-yellow bumblebee. It was so persistent! Every time I swatted it away, it became more and more determined to swoop down on me.

I tried to subtly pick up my pace and trot down the long line of parked cars to get to that store entrance, but it followed me! I guess it was attracted to my perfume and brightly colored clothes. "Buzz, buzz, buzz!" It was getting more aggressive, so I started to panic and swing my arms all around as if I was fighting the air. Just when I thought it was gone, it started flying toward me full-on, straight toward my face. I flung up my arms and started running backward, screaming. I was so excited and running backward so fast that I lost my footing and fell backward with so much force that I slid.

Once that thick polyester material made contact with the concrete it stuck like Velcro, but I kept sliding. I slid right out of my pants. I dropped my purse, my wig fell off, my shoes fell off, and there I lay, right in between two parked cars, spread-eagle like I was on a cross.

An older gentleman walked by, and I thought he was going to help me up, but he just paused, looked down at me, and shook his head in disgust. Hahaha! He must've thought I was some drunk or a crazy person who was off her meds, I guess. So, he just kept right on walking.

I lay there for a second and eventually got up. I pulled my pants up, grabbed my purse and slung it on my shoulder, picked up my wig and shoved it on my head, and put my shoes on. I dusted myself off then politely did an about-face back to my car, got in, and drove home.

No freshly cooked dinner for us. Hot dogs and pork and beans were on the table that night. Later that evening, I called up one of my girlfriends and told her what happened. All she could do was laugh and ask, "Elizabeth, how big was this bee that it would make you get undressed for it, right in the middle of a grocery store parking lot?" Ha ha!

There isn't much that makes me lose my cool, but that bee certainly did.

*****

I consider myself to be a firm, straightforward type of person, but I also believe that you can't take life too seriously. I choose to surround myself with people who have lighthearted personalities.

I had a cousin named Mamie who was just like that. She kind of reminded you of that Aunt Esther character on TV. She looked very similar to her but much younger, quite a bit darker in complexion, and a much less sanctified way of speaking. To some, she came across harsh and loud, but she also had a great sense of humor and a sharp wit. She wasn't afraid to say whatever came to her mind.

I remember her telling me of one time when she and our other cousin were out shopping at a department store, and they got into a debate over who was the blackest, as far as skin tone was concerned, between the two of them. So, Mamie decided to ask someone for an unbiased split vote. She tapped an unassuming white woman on the shoulder and asked her, "Excuse me, ma'am. Between the two of us, who would you say is the blackest?" She said that the look on that woman's face was priceless. I know that woman probably couldn't believe that she would ask her something like that.

I loved Mamie! She was never bothered by what anyone had to say about her. As a matter of fact, Mamie used to always say, "When

I die, I want them to bury me facedown so the whole world can kiss my ass on the way out!" And when she passed a few years later, at her funeral, all my siblings and cousins were lined up with great anticipation in the second and third rows of the church pews…and when they opened the casket, we, all in unison, leaned forward to see if she was actually facedown. She wasn't, but we all sat back and leaned over with muffled laughter in our seats because of what we expected to see. Even in her death, she had us laughing!

*****

Aurora chuckled. "I'm sure it would've been difficult to muffle your laughter had she really been face down in her casket."

"Yes, ma'am. I don't know if I would've been able to contain myself!"

"Elizabeth, it's almost time for the doctors to make their morning rounds, so I'll be back later to sit with you some more, okay?"

"Oh, okay. I know you must be tired sitting there in that hard chair listening to me all night. I'm gonna see my kids today hopefully, so I can talk with them about me getting out of here."

She put her hands on my shoulder. "Just rest, dear. Don't worry yourself. In time, you'll be able to get some clarity about what's going on. Trust me."

# CHAPTER EIGHT

# I Didn't Want to Miss a Single Day

Another day here in this new facility has come and gone, and the craziest part is I don't remember any of what might've occurred today, it's a blur. I guess I slept through everything again! My goodness! I guess I'll catch someone from the nursing staff at some point to see if they can take me off this medicine so I can be alert during the day and get my kids on the phone so I can talk to them and get some answers. Wait, the door is opening…it's Aurora. I'm still trying to figure her out. She's definitely a good listener, if nothing else.

"Hello, my dear. I'm back again to sit with you. Are you up to telling me more of your story?"

Honestly, I'm more concerned with what my future holds at that moment than telling her about my past. But I don't want to be rude or put my issues of concern on her.

"Sure, have a seat. Let's wrap everything up tonight because if I have it my way, I don't plan on being here tomorrow night."

*****

Once my daughter turned a year old, I was scheduled to return to work with the state unemployment office. I really loved working there and didn't want to miss a day because something funny was happening all the time. The claimants were what made the job fun. I mean I would hear tall tales almost every day.

See, in order to maintain benefits, a person must indicate that they are able and available to work. Also back then, things weren't all electronic like they are now. Back then, a person's benefits were given to them by cutting an actual check right there in the office, but each person was usually issued their benefits on a certain day. However, we did make some exceptions for extreme situations. So, you can imagine that there was always somebody with an excuse as to why they needed their benefits early.

A certain young man looked familiar to me. He had been there another time asking for expedited benefits. His excuse this time was that his mother had passed away, and he needed his benefits issued early so he could help pay for her funeral costs. After he shared his excuse, I sat back in my chair and thought for a minute on how I would respond. I looked him dead in his eyes.

"No disrespect, sir. But how many times is your mama going to die?"

There was a few seconds of silence, then he sheepishly put his head down because he knew he had been found out.

"You've been in here once before saying the same thing. And I know for certain that your mama ain't died, came back to life, and died again."

His reply was simple and to the point. "Huh. Yeah, well, all right then. I guess I'll be back next week to get my check on my regular scheduled day."

I just shook my head. "Have a good day, sir."

And, oh my goodness, the one day I missed work, I went back in the following day, and everybody was coming over to my desk telling me that I missed what happened the day before.

We had a coworker named Pat Sledge. She was a very pretty woman; however, she didn't wear traditional women's clothing. She often wore more masculine attire to work, and she kept her hair cut in a short, tapered natural. I could care less about her way of dress or anything else she did for that matter. But there were a few people in the office who would gossip about her and say that they believed she was gay. And some even took it a step further to say that they believed she was having an affair with one of our other coworkers.

It was my opinion that what a person did on their own time, in private, shouldn't be any of our business. But workplace gossip is a difficult foe to contend with, for anyone. Perception is so many people's reality, even if it is distorted.

I heard that the day before, word had gotten back to Pat from another coworker who overheard one of the male supervisors, Mr. Dunnigan, mentioning to a worker in the break room that he believed Pat Sledge was sleeping with the office clerk, Juanita Cosby. Supposedly, he was going on and on about how disgusting they were and that they both should be ashamed of themselves. Well, apparently, Pat had heard rumors before about her off-the-clock activities, and it was at that moment that she had decided she'd had enough.

I was told that when Pat heard the news, she slammed the drawer closed on the file cabinet next to her desk and marched past four long rows of workers sitting at their desks, right over to Supervisor Dunnigan's office. She pounded on his door until he opened it. Then she grabbed him by his suit tie and dragged him up and down each row of workers.

"You wanted to know if I'm gay, right? And you care so much that you want to know who you think I'm screwing. Well, let's see if you can pick them out from among your staff."

They tell me he was hollering. "Let me go, or I'm going to have you fired for insubordination!"

"Well, I guess my gay ass will be standing in one of them lines out front because I ain't letting you go until you figure out who you think I've been sleeping with."

She continued to drag him up and down the rows until they finally got to the back of the fiscal unit where Ms. Cosby was sitting. They said Ms. Cosby was crying and pleading for Ms. Sledge to let Mr. Dunnigan go. Pat Sledge started shouting louder at that point, drowning out Ms. Cosby's pleas.

"What you think, Dunnigan? Do you think it might be her? I'm sure if you get close enough to her and take a good whiff, like the dog you are, you might smell my scent on her."

Then they say she let go of his tie, marched back to her desk, snatched up her belongings, and stormed out. I didn't see her again after that. But I heard that instead of being fired, management decided to just transfer her to another district office.

There was something always going on in that office. I recall an incident where I had to handle a crazy claimant who had come into the office. This lady had gotten fired from her job, so she had to wait thirteen weeks, as a penalty for being fired, before she could collect her unemployment money. Every day that the lady came through the front door, she would cuss out everybody and complain about not being able to get a check. And all the clerks on the counter were afraid of her because she looked like a burly-built man. Well, on this particular day, she had to come in to sign up so that she could start getting her biweekly checks. And my supervisor asked me to go to the front counter to serve her because all the clerks were afraid of her, and she knew I could handle her.

I went up to the counter, and when she got to me, I asked her the standard required questions. And she gave the appropriate responses, no problem. I also informed her that she would have to wait to receive her initial check, and she seemed to understand. I had her fill out the forms, and I thought she was going to just go on and leave. But she walked down to the other end of the counter to the check machine operator and confronted the lady who writes the checks. She asked her why she couldn't just get her check today. The check machine lady told her that she couldn't give an explanation. And if she wanted one, she would have to come back to the line she had been in and have me explain it to her again. So, she came back, and I told her the same thing all over again.

She blurted out, "I ain't trying to hear all that! If you don't give me my check today, I'm kicking your ass! Plain and simple!"

I replied. "Try it, and I'll stump you like a mud puddle!"

Then I stood up and made a grand announcement to the entire front lobby. "Everybody who wants to be paid, please, step over to the next line. 'Cuz I'm fixin' to stump a mudhole in this heifer's ass!"

She replied, "I'm going to jump over this counter and kick your ass!"

I chuckled with great confidence and said, "And you gon' die... in midair."

Little did she know that I had my trusty dagger, about three inches long, hidden in my bra. She proceeded to come around the counter, and the security guard came running over and tried to stop her. He put his hand on her shoulder to hold her back.

"Sir, sir, please…"

I interrupted him. "That ain't no sir! That's a bitch!"

Then I turned to her and said, "If you put your hands on me today, you're going to die today. And if I don't get you here, I'll certainly get you later. Don't forget, I know where you live!"

She stood there in amazement that I would say such a thing to her out loud. The supervisor ran up, and both he and the security guard escorted her right on out the front door. Then the supervisor came telling me that I overreacted.

I told him, "Nah, I ain't overreact because I didn't do nothing to her. And she threatened me. And ain't nobody putting they hands on me. I ain't gon' take it from no man, and I sure ain't gon' take from no woman!"

The next week, when I knew she was scheduled to come back, I purposely sat in that same spot at the front counter. And I had my gun with me that week in my purse and the dagger in my bosom, but no one knew except one person. I told one of the other supervisors, who I was cool with, what I had on me. And I instructed her that if anything happened to me to call my husband.

I probably should've been fired, but I was such a good worker. Hahaha! And that's no lie. I was such an efficient worker that every district office in the city of Detroit wanted me to come and work there to help clear up their backlog. I had an excellent reputation for getting things done much faster than anyone they knew. But anyway, thankfully, she didn't cause a scene that day. She simply collected her check and went on her way.

Months later, I was given the title of assistant supervisor. But I called it flunky supervisor because they seemed to give me the responsibility of handling the claimants who were difficult to deal with.

Another incident came about on a day that I was out in the lobby. To expedite things and help clear out the lobby, I decided to collect the forms from the folks standing in line, go pull their records, and have everything ready for the clerks so we could get them out the door faster. A lady, who so happened to have moved here from Chicago, was standing in the wrong line. It was the payment line, and it was extremely long. It reached all the way back to the entry door.

I politely told her, "Ma'am, you're in the wrong line. It's only about five people over there in the interstate line. And that's the line you're supposed to be in."

"Don't you tell me where I need to be, you big, fat, three-hundred-and-some-odd-pound heifer!"

Just as loud as I could, I whipped back with my response, "And so is your ignorant ass, mammy!

All the claimants in the line, including all the clerks at the counter, fell out laughing. She got embarrassed because everyone was laughing at my response to her. So, she stormed out the door and about thirty minutes later returned with her mama!

The door to the lobby flung open and in comes the two of them with the mama in the lead. And because pretty much every one of us clerks who sat at the lobby counter was fat, the mama started down at the wrong end, confronting each fat clerk, one at a time. The two of them eventually made it down to me. And when they did, I looked at them both and shook my head.

"I knew it had to be two of y'all. The apple sure don't fall too far from the tree!"

She demanded to speak to my supervisor. Now my supervisor was a stone-cold alcoholic, but he'd get himself together whenever he had to deal with the claimants directly. He went out there to talk with them and told them, "If you want respect, you have to show respect." He got them served, and they left. And me and my supervisor went into his office and laughed about the whole thing.

That place was so much fun. And I formed a lot of lasting friendships from all my years working for the state. There was one who worked with me when I was assigned to work in the fraud detection unit on the boulevard. She had been married at least three or four times. And when she had been wronged by any of them, she'd do something crazy revengeful, ultimately ending in divorce.

The first husband had been caught cheating. When she found out, she tossed all his clothes, one by one, out the upstairs bedroom window. His clothes were hanging all over the front yard tree like Christmas ornaments. His underwear, shirts, pants, whatever, each had its own branch. She said it took him at least two hours to get all his clothes out that tree. He had to climb up and down his ladder so much that the neighbors formed a small crowd to watch, point, and laugh. He moved out after that incident and thus started the pattern of marriages and divorces.

A few years later, she met and married her second husband. He wasn't a cheater, but he was a big gambler and compulsive spender. He bought all kinds of expensive shoes. He loved shoes so much that he had a pair to match every suit and outfit he had. She painfully tolerated his spending habits, but one month, he had gone too far and gambled away the money that was to be used for their mortgage. And she wasn't going to tolerate that. One day when he was at work, she called off from work and stayed home to carry out yet another fantastic revenge plot. She gathered up all his shoes and took them out to the garage and used his electric circular saw to cut off the toes of each pair of his shoes, one by one. The marriage didn't last too long after that.

The third husband had been warned of the other two's track records, but I guess he thought he was slicker and smarter than them. However, he soon found out that he wasn't. He got it the worst of them all. He, like the first one, was cheating on her too. She found out about his affair and learned it was with one of her family members. They got into a huge fight, and he hit her.

She let a few days go by, and one day, he fell asleep on the couch after drinking a few beers. She waited until he started snoring and took the lamp that was on the end table next to the couch and cracked him over the head with it. She hit him so hard that it knocked him unconscious because he didn't wake up. Then she unzipped his pants and pulled out his man part. She got herself some super glue and stretched out his appendage as much as she could so that it lay flat and straight. She then glued it to his belly so that the tip was pointing in the direction of his face. Ha! Oh my goodness! I can only imagine what it took for him to loosen himself from that glue so he could pee without it shooting straight up toward his face!

I can't recall if she married anyone else after that last one, but I hate to think what might've happened to the next dude if she did.

Some of the most fun I've ever had was when I was at work or when I hung out with a few of the ladies outside of work. One coworker turned close friend had the same first name as me and a very similar last name. We became very close and even traveled together with our kids. She was one of my very best friends, all the way up until the day she passed away.

She had gotten violently ill one day when she was at my house. We rushed her to the hospital where she stayed overnight for testing. It turned out that she was experiencing kidney failure. She eventually had to go on dialysis. But that didn't stop us from still hanging and traveling together. She lived a long time with that condition until she passed away at age eighty just a few years ago. I miss her so much it hurts to even talk about it.

But anyway…yes, indeed, it was truly a pleasure to work with her and all the other lively characters at the unemployment office. I didn't want to miss a single day.

# CHAPTER NINE

# *Time Brings About a Change*

You really should be grateful for every good little thing that happens in life because you never know when the rough times are coming. And they most assuredly come when you least expect it.

In the summer of 1980, my oldest son was working, had moved out, and had even gotten married. My middle boy was still a preteen, and my daughter was eight years old. I was forty-eight and my husband, Joshua, was eighty-one at this point. Due to his age, he had completely stopped working, so he was the one at home during the time that the children were out of school. He was such a loving and caring father, and the kids loved being at home with him, especially in the summertime.

He'd get up every day and fix the kids a nice big breakfast. Then about noon, they could go out and play with their friends. Also, he made it his business to go on walks with Sheryl almost every day. And at the end of each walk, they'd make a stop at the candy store, and he'd buy her favorite apple-flavored hard candy and a bag of onion-flavored puffs shaped like little onion rings. This was her absolute most favorite treat combination. More than the treats, Sheryl enjoyed the daily routine of stopping by the vegetable market with Joshua where the cashiers would *ooh* and *aww* over how cute she was and marvel at the fact that Joshua had such a young child.

Sheryl was totally a daddy's girl. She loved the pretend pony rides that Joshua would give her on his back, the weekly storybook times, and an occasional cup of coffee that he would fix so that the two of them could sit and sip while they watched the daytime game shows. Even at his age, he was more fit and had more vitality than most men thirty years his junior.

Joshua was very active with Darryl as well. He accompanied Darryl on his daily newspaper route and kept him active with karate lessons and various sports. Truth be told, I am so grateful to the Lord above for allowing me to have met and married Joshua. Although things weren't always perfect within our union, I acknowledge that God's grace is what kept us together for so long. He was always supportive and understanding. We hardly ever got into a disagreement, and when we did, we agreed to always be respectful of one another. He loved me unconditionally, and I loved him just as much. Even during the times within our marriage when I was young and foolish, he dealt with me and covered me through some very shaky moments. But he never made me feel less than or held any fault against me. I was truly blessed.

Sometime in June or July of 1980, Joshua was diagnosed with prostate cancer. He was devastated. Although the doctor had given him a fairly positive prognosis, Joshua allowed the news to take over his outlook on life. He went from being an active, vibrant person to eventually needing twenty-four-hour care.

Early on, he didn't want to accept what was told to him by the doctor. However, eventually, he accepted that he was getting worse, but sadly he didn't want to fight it. He went from home care to nursing home care to being back at home and, lastly, the hospital. I visited him every day and took the kids with me several times a week. My oldest, Joshua Jr., was a big support to me because he took it upon himself to step in and help with the two younger ones.

My sister, Doris, was also very supportive and would come and get the kids and take them to the community center for activities such as swimming, sports, and crafts. Doris's husband, Eugene, and Joshua had formed a brotherhood bond over the years, and the mechanics of their relationship shifted too. The two of them used to sit and talk, over a couple of beers, about sports, politics, religion, and whatever. And often, Eugene would purposefully rile up Joshua just for fun, especially over the subject of politics.

Joshua hardly ever got heated about anything. But politics was always a hot-button topic for him. No matter how intense their discussions became, Eugene would say something clever or humorous to disturb the seriousness of the conversation, and they both would fall out laughing. And Joshua would say, "Man, you sure are crazy." But now, it seemed that no amount of exciting conversation could make Joshua feel any better. And I could tell that it was affecting Eugene emotionally.

It had been about a year since his diagnosis when I got a phone call from Darryl while I was at work. He was crying, and I could hear him consoling Sheryl while trying to form the right words to tell me what was wrong. I knew Joshua was in the hospital and Joshua Jr. was at work, so I was eager to know what could be upsetting both of them to the point of tears.

Darryl was thirteen, so I allowed him to watch his sister during the day while they were on summer break. The neighbor across the street was a stay-at-home mother, and our families were very close. So, she offered to keep a watch on the kids and assured me that if anything happened, she would intervene and contact me immediately. Since I hadn't heard from her, I was hoping that Darryl was calling me because of something minor.

Unfortunately, that was not the case. The hospital had called the house, and since Darryl was the one to answer the phone, they informed him that their father, my husband, had just passed away. When Darryl finally mustered up the wherewithal to tell me the reason why he was calling me and crying, my heart sank into my shoes.

My ears started ringing, and it felt like at that moment the time had stopped. I was at my desk at work, surrounded by ringing phones and loud coworkers, but it felt like I was on a deserted island or floating aimlessly through space all alone. I knew Joshua was getting worse, but my heart wouldn't let me accept the fact that my husband would no longer be with me. My children would no longer have their father, and I was…I don't know what I was. Numb, I guess, is the best way to describe how I felt.

We laid my beloved husband to rest in July 1981. Doris's husband, Eugene, had a heart attack and passed away just three months later. By the end of that year, both Doris and I were widows left with young children to raise. The transition was extremely difficult. We all had to deal with this great loss. From that point forward, we made it a priority to have as much combined family time as possible. We spent every holiday together.

That first Christmas without our husbands, we decided to have a family sleepover at my house. Doris brought over her two kids, Diane and little Eugene. My kids, Darryl and Sheryl, were happy to have their cousins there, and it was a healthy distraction from the fact that they were missing their father. We all put on our pajamas, and I got out my Christmas albums and record player. We played games together and drank hot chocolate while listening to Christmas music. It was the beginning of many life changes to come.

One major and necessary change for me was to start going back to church. My faith in God had not gone away. I guess I just allowed life situations to distract me from what was most important. I needed to refocus as well as expose my children to a lifestyle that placed God at the forefront. They not only needed to go to church, but it was important to me that each developed their own personal relationship with the Lord.

I made it my business to get them up and dressed every Sunday morning. We started going to a nondenominational church, Maranatha Christian Assembly. The name intrigued me, so I looked up the meaning and found that the word Maranatha means "Christ is coming." I thought it clever that part of the message of the gospel of Christ was within the name of the church.

The kids seemed to enjoy going, and I eventually found myself becoming more and more involved in church activities and gatherings. Marla started attending services with me too, and we both eventually joined as members after attending for several months.

The pastor of the church was a very charismatic, middle-aged black man named Walter Watkins. He and his wife, Patricia, a significantly younger white woman, moved here from Minnesota a couple of years prior to start a new life in Michigan. The Watkins had a twin boy and girl named Jackson and Wanda. And they were a couple of years younger than my daughter. They all took a liking to each other and became quite close. After being at the church for a little while, I took notice that the children were wearing the same clothes quite often. I discreetly had a conversation with the pastor's wife and offered some of my kids' clothes that didn't fit anymore. I was a little nervous because I didn't want to offend her, but she was very appreciative.

She and I gradually formed a friendship to where I had even started having them all over to the house for dinner after church. This started to become a regular thing. And once people started hearing about the meals that I was preparing, they wanted an opportunity to put their feet under Elizabeth Roman's table. I started inviting others, and there were some weeks that I would have upward of twenty people at my house to enjoy a good meal.

One Sunday, I decided to scale back because I was tired and just didn't feel like a house full of folks that day. There were only two families I invited that Sunday. Pastor Watkins, his wife, and kids, and Marla and her second husband, Wilson. Unfortunately, Marla and Wilson didn't make it because she had to go pick him up from his cousin's house. He was over there playing cards and drinking the night before. He had gotten so drunk that they wouldn't allow him to drive home. So, Marla had to leave right after church and go retrieve him. I'm sure that she had a few words for him because it was becoming a norm, and she was tired of it.

That Sunday dinner with the Watkins was a laid back one. After we all ate, the kids went to the basement to play while Pastor Watkins, his wife, and I kicked back and enjoyed some after-dinner coffee. Pastor Watkins had his feet propped up on the ottoman and was scanning my living room.

"Sister Roman, you certainly have a lovely home."

"Thank you, Pastor."

"Yes, indeed, a very lovely home. I certainly hope one day to be able to obtain such a nice home for my family. Patricia and I have been so focused on trying to build the ministry that we've had to put other things on the back burner. But I'm trusting God that one day soon we'll be able to afford to purchase a nice home for our children here in Michigan."

"Oh, yeah? Well, I'm sure once the membership grows a little more, you'll have the help you need to free up time to focus more on the needs of your family."

"Yeah, I wish that was the only issue. It's not just the lack of time that's a problem. It's a lack of finances. I'm trying to put the ministry in a position so that we can get out of that storefront and into an actual church building. However, the other members aren't as faithful as you, Sister Roman. Folks aren't giving in the offerings enough to maintain what we have, let alone enough to move into a building we can eventually own. I certainly wish we had more members like you."

I didn't really know how to respond to that. I wasn't looking for any type of acknowledgment or accolades. I was only doing what I was taught to do from childhood. I remember my parents serving in the church and giving in the offerings no matter how little they had. My father always instilled in us the importance of having a giving heart and a servant's heart as a member of the body of Christ.

"Pastor, do you think that maybe folks just aren't aware of what your mission is? And maybe this is why they aren't motivated to give and support."

"No. Unfortunately, I have expressed my vision and pleaded with them for their support, and it's like pulling teeth trying to get them to see what I see. We could be a great benefit to the community, and to the membership as a whole, if people would step up a little bit more. I have grown somewhat weary, but I refuse to give up. Because when Patricia and I come across folks like you and Marla, we become a bit more hopeful. All in all, I believe the Lord will provide."

"Amen, Pastor, amen. It'll get better soon. We just have to keep the faith."

After being at Maranatha for a little over a year, it was becoming more evident to me that what Pastor Watkins had expressed to me some months prior was painfully true. The majority of the members at the church didn't want to help or contribute much. Those who were active and supportive were getting burnt out, and I personally was getting more and more frustrated with the mindset of many of the members as well. I often overheard people complaining about this or that. But they never had any suggestions as to how to make things better.

One Sunday, my kids and I stayed back to help straighten up after the morning service. I noticed that most of the men of the church rushed out right after service so they could make it home in time to watch football. That left me, my kids, Marla, Pastor Watkins, and his family and a couple other members to break down and lock up the equipment, straighten chairs, and pick up trash in preparation for next week. I could see the frustration on Patricia's face. I'm sure she would've loved to be more of a traditional first lady and have people available to handle the more laborious tasks of the church so that she could concentrate on the operational needs a bit more. I saw for myself how hard she worked and how little help she was getting, even from those who were considered her close confidantes.

I reached out and put my hand on her shoulder in an attempt to offer her some comfort. When she turned around to face me, I saw tears welling up in her eyes. I took her hand and pulled her into the restroom to see what was wrong although I had some idea.

"What's the matter, sweetheart? Why are you upset?"

She responded through tears. "Walter and I are about to lose this place. We haven't been able to keep current on the rent, and we're behind by about two thousand dollars. Walter and I have come to the point now that we have even considered moving back to Minnesota because we can't keep things going here. I just don't know what to do."

I tried to give her some encouragement. "Sister Patricia, I can't pretend to know how you're feeling. But one thing I do know is that when you're feeling like you're at your lowest point and you feel like giving up, you have to find strength to keep going. Especially if you truly believe that God has commissioned you to see a thing through. I'm sure that if we hold some sort of fundraiser or something that you all will have enough to pay the back rent. Maybe you can run it by him and see what he says."

She looked up from crying into her tissue. "Thank you so much, Sister Elizabeth. I appreciate you more than you know. I'll talk with Walter. We have until the end of this month to come up with something. So, we have at least three weeks to make something happen. I'm sure the Lord will provide."

"Yeah, the Lord will provide, but these folks need to step up and allow the Lord to use them in this process as well. Faith without works is dead. But don't worry, I believe things will turn around. Stay encouraged. Don't give up yet."

That next Sunday, Pastor and Sister Watkins stood at the front of the church after service and made the announcement that we would be holding a bake sale the following Saturday. They asked that every member donate two or three baked good items and for us to invite as many people as we could to come out and support.

I made four pineapple cream cheese pies. The pies were always a big hit at any gathering I held at my home, so I was confident that they would sell easily at the bake sale. Marla made a huge hotel serving pan of her famous peach cobbler to donate to the bake sale as well.

That Saturday, there were about twenty to thirty members who actually showed up with cakes, pies, and cookies to help out with the sale. And if I had to guess, I'd say we had about a hundred or more people show up to buy the baked goods. It looked like we might make our goal of raising the money for the back rent on the building.

Two days after the bake sale, I got a phone call from Patricia Watkins. She asked if she and her husband could stop by my house because they wanted to speak with me. I was eager because I anticipated that they had good news about the results of the bake sale and wanted to share it with me in person. When they arrived, I invited them in to have a seat in the living room. Since they didn't have their children with them, I asked Sheryl to go up to her room and occupy herself until my guests were gone.

I tried to read their faces, but I couldn't make out if they had good news or bad news. I offered them a cup of coffee. They declined. Pastor Watkins thanked me for allowing them to drop by without much notice.

"Sister Roman, let me start off by saying that we did pretty well with the bake sale Saturday."

"Oh! That's wonderful."

"But…the money we collected, along with Sunday's offering, only got us just past the halfway point of what we need. Unless we come up with an additional seven hundred, we'll still have to vacate. Which means I'll have to close down the church this Sunday and pack up my family and move on back to Minnesota. My brother says he can get me a job at the furniture store he manages, and we will have to figure out our next move later on down the road."

I sat in silence for a moment, not really knowing how to appropriately respond. I wasn't sure if I should offer some encouraging words or if I should just wait to see if Patricia had anything to add. Just when I was preparing my words, Patricia spoke up.

"Sister Elizabeth, this is probably one of the most difficult and humbling positions to be in. And in any other situation, we would not ever think to ask you this, but we are prayerfully hoping that you will allow us to borrow the money, that's if you are able. We would be so grateful. We promise to pay you back by the end of next month. This would help us settle the debt with the owner of the building and free us from having to let go of everything we have worked so hard to accomplish with the ministry and our lives here in Michigan."

I continued to sit in silence. How could they assume that I would have that kind of money to let them borrow? How could they assume that our relationship was such that I would be willing to extend that kind of courtesy to them? I was sure that they were making such a request out sheer desperation. But what I wasn't sure of was whether they could get seven hundred dollars back into my hands by the end of the next month. If they couldn't afford to come up with the money all this time, how were they going to get it by next month?

Patricia started crying, and Walter reached over to console her. I continued to sit in silence, contemplating how to respond. I felt empathetic, but I had been burned by people before, and I certainly didn't want to be burned again, especially not by a pastor.

Against my better judgment, I agreed to help. But on the condition that they would give me details as to their plan of repayment and sign a promissory note.

They explained that they would sell one of their old cars, both of their fur coats, and whatever else they needed to sell or pawn and assured me that they would have enough to repay me by next month and make next month's rent. But they needed my help now to make sure that they met the landlord's deadline for this month.

"As you both know, my husband passed away. I don't have anyone other than myself to keep things afloat in my home. When he died, I had just enough to pay the funeral expenses and to pay off our car loan. And to give you an even clearer picture, the company for which he worked claims that they never received the paperwork we sent in for me to receive his pension. So, I'm making ends meet just on survivor's benefits for the kids and my income from my job. I'm telling you all of this because I need you both to understand that I *need* my money back by the end of next month—no exceptions."

Patricia began to cry even harder, but those tears were tears of relief and gratitude. Pastor Watkins grabbed my hands and began to thank me profusely. I politely slid my hands from his and added my last words of warning. "I know that you both are good people, but I need to let you know that I have been done wrong quite a few times in my past, and I don't want our relationship to be tarnished. I need you both to understand that I'm expecting my money back, and if there is an issue with me getting it back by the date you say, it will be a major issue."

They both assured me in no uncertain terms that they would keep their word.

The following Sunday was a wonderful service. Pastor Watkins spoke about faith and trusting in God during difficult life situations. I felt honored that I was able to help them with things to keep the ministry going although I'd be lying if I said I wasn't still a little nervous about it all. I worked through my nerves while I helped to put away the chairs after service. Pastor Watkins finished up the weekly after-service meet and greets, and he came over to offer a hand.

He thanked me again for my help and said, "God is gonna bless you real good for your faithfulness, Sister Roman."

I thanked him for his kind words and finished up.

Two weeks had gone by, and the end of the month was a couple of weeks away. I was trying my best to maintain my nerves. That Sunday, I wasn't able to stay after service and help with the cleanup. I went to look for Patricia to let her know that I had an engagement right after church that I needed to attend. Her demeanor was somewhat dry, and she wasn't giving me the same warm smile that she normally did. It made me a little uneasy, but I brushed it off and told myself that I was just hypersensitive because of what we discussed regarding the money I loaned them, and the deadline was approaching. But I decided to throw away my negative thoughts and headed out the door to my next engagement.

It was difficult over the next couple of days to keep my negative thoughts at bay regarding the money I loaned the Watkins. My anxiety was growing as the deadline for repayment grew closer. Wednesday or Thursday of that week, my friend Marla called me with some unbelievable news. She didn't even give me time to say hello before she started out.

"Girl! You ain't gon' never guess what I just found out!"

"What?"

"Take a guess!"

"Girl, I don't have time to play no guessing games. Just tell me!"

"Okay, okay! Girl, Deacon Moore just called and told me that Pastor Watkins and Sister Watkins have left town."

My heart started to race. "What! What do you mean left town? For good?"

"Yes, girl! For good. Can you believe that? How they just gonna pack up and leave and not say nothing to nobody? I mean that's crazy!"

I didn't bother to give a response. "Listen, let me call you back. I need to call around and find out what's going on."

Marla didn't know that I had allowed them to borrow money, and I planned on keeping it that way. I was shocked, angry, and hurt, all at the same time. I was thinking that this couldn't possibly be true. I had to speak with Deacon Moore myself! Well, I came to find out after doing so that it was true. Pastor Watkins had given the church over to one of the ministers on staff to run, and he moved with his family back to Minnesota without a single word to me. I was so hot I felt like my head was going to shoot off my shoulders like a rocket.

I tried calling select members of the church who I thought would have a way of getting in touch with him. I finally got my hands on the phone number for the minister who was supposed to be taking over. He told me that Pastor Watkins's leave was only temporary. He planned to go back to his hometown and find work, save up for about a year, and then return to Michigan to take back the church.

Pastor Watkins had been gone for about a month, and I continued to attend church services so I could stay connected with the new pastor long enough to coax a contact number out of him for the Watkins family, which I did.

I stared at the phone number for a few minutes with the phone receiver in my hand. I held the receiver for so long, gazing at the number, that I heard a loud rhythmic beep, beep, beep, letting me know that the phone was off the hook for too long. I held my finger down on the button to allow the phone to reset in preparation for me to dial. I methodically dialed (612) 555-****. The phone rang several times, and I was just about to hang up...

Someone picked up. "Hello?"

I hesitated for a split second. "Yes. Hello...may I speak to Walter Watkins, please?"

The person on the other end said, "This is Mrs. Watkins. How may I help you?"

I had to tell myself to be cool. "Hi, Patricia. This is Elizabeth."

There was a short silence...

"Oh, uh, hello, Sister Elizabeth. Uh, Walter isn't in at the moment. But I can assume you're calling regarding the money. Uh, is it okay if I have him call you this evening when he gets in?"

"Well, to be quite honest with you, Patricia, it would've been nice to get a call from either of you a couple of weeks ago before you both decided to skip town without repaying me my money. And now you're telling me that I need to wait until he gets home in order to get an explanation? This is crazy. You can't tell me what's going on? I would hate to think you both were being dishonest with me and had intended on keeping my money all along. So, what? Y'all used my money to help you relocate?"

"No, no, no. That's not it at all. Elizabeth, please let me—"

"Let you what? Come up with another lie?"

"Now let me assure you that we had no intention of keeping your money. It's just that we were not able to get all the money from selling our things. So, Walter figured if we came back to Minnesota and he got a job, which he did, then we could pay you back in full by the end of this month. I thought he had spoken with you about this before we left."

"Honestly, Patricia, I find it hard to believe that you didn't know that he didn't speak to me about it. And in any case, I spoke to both of you and told you good that I wanted my money back by the end of last month. So, what makes you think that I would change my mind so quickly on the issue? I tell you what. You let your husband know that if I don't hear from him this evening and I don't get my money by the end of this week, y'all are going to have a problem on your hands!"

I never received a call from him. And after several weeks of trying to make contact with him, I had come to the conclusion that I was never going to see my money again. The thought of this hurt me to my core. It took a lot for me to even trust this so-called man of faith. I have had so many people try to take advantage of my kindness over the years. I have had to struggle and overcome quite a bit in my life, and that is why it's really hard not to be closed off to people. I wish I could've gotten into my car and driven all the way to Minnesota to find the two of them. The anger I was feeling was very strong, and I wanted to show them my wrath!

I finally confessed to Marla what happened, and she helped me get past it. She reminded me of the scripture that talks about vengeance being the Lord's to handle. She helped me to let it go, and eventually I did. Years later, I was even able to totally forgive them. It took some time, but I had to release it. I couldn't expect God to forgive me if I couldn't forgive who had hurt me.

That was a hard lesson to learn. I grew a great deal from that experience. But, thankfully, it didn't tarnish my thoughts about God or serving his people. After all, Walter Watkins was just a man—plain and simple. And like any other man, he had flaws. I had concluded that Walter Watkins and his wife were obviously desperate. So much so that they had resorted to theft. And after truly thinking about that, my anger was replaced with compassion. And I grew to understand that my relationship with God could not be affected by any other person's negative actions. I had to learn to focus my attention on the Lord and love his people, even in their faults, because I sure enough had plenty of my own. That's what you call agape, godly, unconditional love.

God has been so good to me throughout the years. He blessed me with an awesome husband and wonderful children. He blessed me with a beautiful home and a stable job. And in all my years since I made my burnt offering covenant with him, I have not seen a single day of hunger or lack. As a matter of fact, I have been blessed beyond my expectations. So much so that God has used me to bless others. I have been able to give away groceries, clothes, furniture, and, even on one occasion, a car to people in my life who exhibited a real need. I have had whole families temporarily move into my home with me and my daughter, and I wouldn't charge them a dime so that they could save enough to be able to afford a place of their own.

I wouldn't change a thing about my life because my past helped me develop into who I am today. And because I know what it's like to feel unloved and to be without the basic necessities, I feel compelled to give to others in need. Yes, there are those here and there who try to take advantage, but I won't let that stop me. My promise to God will not be broken just because of a few "takers." My heart is always open to show compassion, and I will never let anyone or anything change that!

A year or two after the Walter Watkins incident, Marla and I eventually found another church home. It was a small fellowship on the east side of Detroit. We both served faithfully and were actively involved in many different functions and events that went on there. My daughter, Sheryl, was active with the youth group, and she loved attending this church because there were so many kids there her age.

SHARON ROWLAND

We grew to love the people and often had many of the members over to the house for dinner after church, just like we did with our old church members. We attended all the annual conferences and enjoyed just being around the wonderful people. The Sunday services were always so uplifting and even transformational. I witnessed people receive the Lord as their Savior, be healed from infirmities and physical disablements, be delivered from addictions, be freed from spiritual and emotional strongholds, and it was all so wonderful to see because I grew to know and become friends with some of those very same people.

Sunday after Sunday, I witnessed people going to the altar during Sunday morning service because they may have found themselves in situations that provoked them to seek prayer or help. The pastor would pray over them, and they would walk away with their hands raised in the air and thanking the Lord.

I served at this church for what was going on about five years, and it was at this point that I started noticing a shift. A deacon in the church had fallen into sexual sin and cheated on his wife. The pastor made the two of them stand in front of the entire congregation to "set things right" with him because, as he explained it, the deacon was a church leader and needed to be rebuked publicly.

I didn't agree with the way it was handled. I felt that having this man stand up and expose his sin openly, causing extreme embarrassment to his wife and children, was not the way to deal with it, regardless of the position he had at the church. I thought that the pastor should've dealt with that issue with more discretion and perhaps offered him and his wife some counseling, particularly if he was remorseful.

Unfortunately, they weren't the only ones he had done this with. He started calling others up to the front of the church who had been "found in sin" and publicly shaming them. Instead of showing love and compassion and giving guidance to overcome the guilt and shame, he was doing quite the opposite.

Marla and I were part of a board of women who were respected highly in the church, so we decided that we should perhaps have a meeting with the pastor to offer our thoughts on how this action was

144

affecting those involved. But we got shut down. The pastor didn't want to listen to our perspective and didn't care to consider how this was affecting everyone else.

I eventually bore witness to a lot of things that started changing at that church, things that weren't good. And it started with the pastor. Something in him wasn't the same, and it was only a matter of time before he, too, was exposed. We discovered that the pastor was just as flawed as the folks he openly rebuked from the pulpit.

Eventually, there was a scandal that came out about him. No one, from the administrative staff on down, could believe that he was involved in a long-term indiscretion with a woman who worked at the church as an administrator. It rocked the entire membership, causing the church to split. Over half of the members left after that.

I stopped attending there as well. And once again, I found myself having to look at things from a biblical perspective as opposed to focusing on the actual person. Don't get me wrong, I was hurt and disappointed again by the actions of a man. But the love I had for God was stronger than any psychological or emotional blow I sustained. All I kept telling myself was "This, too, would pass."

# CHAPTER TEN

# We've All Got a Story to Tell

After about three to four years of visiting and searching for a new church home, my daughter, Sheryl, started attending a church, in the city of Southfield, called Dynamic Love Outreach Ministries. By this time, Sheryl was in her early twenties and was able to make her own decisions about where she wanted to fellowship. And after witnessing her enthusiasm and dedication to this fellowship, I decided that I wanted to pay this church a visit. It was headed by a young man and his wife, Pastors Richard and Karla Lansford.

After attending service just one time, I was pleasantly surprised. The praise and worship portion of the service was like no other I had ever experienced before. It was truly a wonderful thing to see so many young men and women come together to glorify God in a fashion that made you want to clear your heart and mind of all distractions and join in. And to see the pastor right there in the middle of it was a refreshing thing to witness.

At most of the churches I visited, the pastor didn't participate in any part of the service until it was time for him to get up to speak. When the choir or worship leaders were singing, the pastor would either be in his office waiting for it to be over, or he'd stay seated as if he was watching a concert on TV, while everyone else would be on their feet joining in. However, to see this pastor not only joining in but intensely giving praise to God made me feel he was a man I could glean something from. But because of my past experiences, I wanted to take my time before aligning myself with any new ministry.

I attended services at Dynamic Love Outreach Ministries weekly for over a year before I decided that I would become a member. And I have had the pleasure of learning from, and growing immensely under, the teachings of Pastor Richard Lansford. Both he and his wife have shown forth an authentic love for God and people. Karla Lansford was raised up in the Church of God in Christ like I was, and she always exhibited the sweetest disposition I have ever had the pleasure to witness.

Pastor Lansford often testified that although his mother was a churchgoing and God-fearing woman in his younger years, he didn't necessarily follow her belief system. He shared how as a teenager he was involved with all kinds of delinquent activity. He also often talked about his shortcomings as a full-grown man, husband, and father.

He used himself as an example in many of his sermons so that people would know he never thought too highly of himself. He wanted people to know that if God could save him, he could save anybody. He had a certain edge to him that let you know he wasn't your average preacher. He was intense and enthusiastic. But he knew the scriptures, and it was very evident that he lived by them as well. I have been a member there from that day to this.

As time passed on, I spent most of my days either going to church, traveling, or relaxing at home. I had been retired from the State of Michigan for about a year, so I had a lot more time on my hands. Marla was retired from her job too, but she was facing some real personal challenges.

Her second husband, Wilson, passed away in 1993. She found him sitting on the living room sofa with the TV remote control still in his hand. I got the call from her around midnight. Sheryl and I went straight over there to sit with her until the coroner came. Marla, Sheryl, and I all sat there in the living room with Wilson's body, talking and carrying on like he was simply sleeping. Marla didn't appear to be traumatized or even upset in the least. And to be honest, neither was I nor Sheryl. Her second chance at marriage wasn't what she had hoped it would be.

Unlike her first husband, he wasn't physically violent toward her, but he did give her a boatload of grief. He cheated on her multiple times, and in addition to that, he was an outright drunk. It had gotten so bad that he would be locked up from being pulled over for driving drunk more times than we could count. I never understood how he kept getting released only to be arrested all over again, time after time. It was not surprising for any of us to find out that cirrhosis of the liver was his cause of death.

About three years after Wilson passed, Marla was diagnosed with Alzheimer's disease. It became noticeable to me when she got disoriented and turned around during our regular weekend shopping trips to our favorite stores in the city of Hamtramck. We visited the same stores and took the same route each time for years, and when I saw that it was becoming increasingly difficult for her to navigate there and back home, I suggested she go to a doctor to get checked out. She initially blew it off and refused to go. Then other things started happening. And her personality even started to change.

She became easily agitated and very snippy. And during one of our out-of-town getaways, she even accused me of plotting to kill her when we were younger. She had this crazy notion that during the time when she stayed with me and my husband, I pulled a knife on her. I was totally floored and hurt by the accusation, and for a little while, we had stopped talking again behind that.

But some moths later, I got a call from her oldest daughter, Brenda. She informed me that she had to escort Marla to the doctor because she was starting to wander off from home, leave the stove on, and things like that. And she was fearful that her mother would eventually cause harm to herself. When I heard the news that she received the Alzheimer's diagnosis, I was sad, and then I understood all the unexplainable changes I saw in my dear friend. It was heartbreaking that I was losing her to this terrible disease, and I decided to make the best of the time we had left together.

A few short years later, Marla's condition worsened to the point that she needed twenty-four-hour care. Brenda was trying her best to take care of Marla but had some medical challenges of her own. The stress from caring for her mother began to take a toll on her.

Brenda eventually had to check herself into the hospital and allow her younger sister, Tracey, to take over for a while. Unfortunately, this was the beginning of the end.

Marla had always known that her youngest daughter, Tracey, was no good. She was a liar, a thief, a drug user, and as trifling as they come. Marla used to say that no matter how sick she got, she would never want Tracey to be her caregiver. But like many stories go, we don't always have control over how things turn out.

Marla stayed with Tracey for not even a full month and passed away—all while Brenda was still hospitalized. Brenda was told what happened to her mother, and two weeks to the day after Marla passed, so did Brenda. It was so sad. We had to have two funerals back-to-back for mother and daughter. After Marla's and Brenda's funerals, I didn't have any more contact with Tracey. Nor did I want to.

By the time Marla passed away, I had been a member of Dynamic Love Outreach Ministries for about fifteen years, and I loved every minute of it. I established lasting relationships with a few of the members, some of whom came from the previous church I attended on the east side. There was one family, the Andrews family, from the previous church that I remained close with, and they eventually joined Dynamic Love Outreach Ministries just a couple years after I did. James Andrews and his wife, Georgia, have four children that I have witnessed grow up from little kids into full-grown adults. And I consider them to be just like family to me.

They have been to my home for Sunday dinners more times than I can count, and I have enjoyed a few meals at their table as well. These last few years, I have truly slowed down with all the Sunday dinners at my home especially since my kids are all grown now. It's hard to believe, but my oldest son, Joshua Jr., is sixty, Darryl is forty-nine, Sheryl just turned forty-four a few days ago, and I'll be eighty-five in a few months. Needless to say, those days of me cooking large meals for twenty to twenty-five folks all crowded up in my home are long gone. However, Sheryl and my sister Doris's daughter, Diane, have been doing really good with hosting the large family dinners on major holidays.

Diane is like a daughter to me, and I am so proud of the woman she has become. She and Sheryl have a special bond. They're more like sisters than cousins. When Sheryl had to stay in the hospital for over a month due to complications from hysterectomy surgery, Diane handled all her personal business while she was in recovery.

I swear, those doctors messed up my baby! They caused more harm than good to her body. She had to undergo six subsequent surgeries to correct the damage they did to her.

Just four days after she had her initial surgery, she was discharged home and woke up in excruciating pain that same night. We discovered later that the doctor nicked her bowel during surgery. From this, she had to undergo exploratory surgery to see what damage was done. They discovered over a liter of fecal matter in her abdominal cavity. She developed sepsis, and her organs were shutting down. She was placed in a medically induced coma for four days to allow her body to rest and, hopefully, begin to recover. Diane was there with me the very next day after Sheryl was readmitted to the hospital.

When she walked into the room and saw Sheryl hooked up to a respirator and all those machines, she broke down crying.

The nurse who was in the room pulled Diane aside. "Hello, dear. How are you related to the patient?"

"I'm her cousin. What happened to her? Why is she like this?"

"Unfortunately, she suffered an injury to her bowel during her first surgery, and it caused her to develop sepsis, then a portion of her lungs collapsed, and currently her kidneys are not functioning to an acceptable level. We're watching her around the clock. We just have to wait and see how she pulls through."

Diane wiped her tears and responded, "Well, I'm trusting God that she's going to be okay."

"Listen, this is serious. She's in bad shape, and we don't know if she's gonna make it. We're not just watching her day by day, we're watching her hour by hour."

"Okay. Well, I don't know what you believe. But we believe in God. And I'm praying, asking God to take care of my cousin. I'm going to have faith and be strong for her. And I hope that whoever is providing care for her will do the same."

When I heard what the nurse told Diane, I started to cry. "I'm going to have to bury my child!"

Diane turned to me. "Auntie, you've got to have faith. We serve a God who is able to do anything."

"You're right…you're right. I'm going to trust God. I have to believe that she's going to be okay."

"Good."

The nurse spoke up, "I'll be here for the next few hours, so please let me know if there's anything you or her mother needs while you're here. I'll be happy to get it. Okay?"

"Yes. Okay. Thank you."

Three days later, Sheryl woke up…and when she awoke, she found herself having to overcome many additional challenges. She had to have a yet another exploratory surgery to figure out why she was experiencing pain in both of her sides. It was discovered that during the second surgical procedure, her bladder developed a hole and was pouring out urine through her rectum. As a result, she then had to wear a urinary catheter for seven months to see if her bladder would heal on its own. It didn't, and she ultimately had to have it repaired.

Sheryl was in ICU and was unable to breathe on her own and was on the ventilator the first two weeks. Afterward, she was finally moved to a regular room where they began to sit her up and let her sit in a chair for a few minutes a day. After being in the hospital for about a month, she began to show improvement to where they trans-ferred her to another location that offered inpatient rehab. She was there for about two and half additional weeks for intense physical and occupational therapy.

Besides having to contend with the catheter, she also had to wear a wound vac to help close an inch-deep incision on the outer layer of her skin. This was to allow the incision to heal from the inside out and close up on its own. Along with that, she still had a colostomy bag and had to drag around an oxygen tank. Sheryl sported these contraptions all while undergoing therapy and recover-ing at home for several weeks thereafter.

Just this past December, three days before Christmas, she went back in to have her bladder repaired. But while there, she suffered yet another complication. Just hours before she was to be discharged to home, she started passing out. Then she developed a level of pain similar to the very first episode. So, once again, we called on everyone to pray as the doctors needed to go back in and find what was wrong.

They discovered that she had a big ball of clotted blood the size of a billiard ball in her abdomen. She had been bleeding internally, and this was what was causing her to pass out and to be in so much pain. The miraculous thing was that they couldn't determine the source of the bleed and how or why the blood clotted, stopping the bleed on its own. But I know why, the prayers to God! The doctors were amazed, and all they could do was just remove the large clot and sew her back up.

She was discharged a few days later and has been home since then. And by the grace of God, she is almost fully recovered. She needs to have one final surgery to reconnect her bowels, and I can't begin to express how nervous I am about it. But I'm going to have to trust God again that she'll be okay.

I am so impressed with my daughter. She has remained strong through it all. And I was at her hospital bedside every single day—thanks to the wonderful folks at my church.

They actually had a rotating schedule among certain members where they would pick me up from my house and carry me down to the hospital to see her every day. And even when Sheryl was in the rehabilitation facility, located forty minutes outside the city, they still saw to it that I got to see her every day! And my daughter's coworkers made out a schedule to have dinner delivered to me every day because they knew Sheryl was the one cooking for me nowadays. The love and support Sheryl and I received was beyond measure. I am so grateful for everyone who stepped in to help.

Just a couple of weeks ago, Sheryl, Diane, and a few other folks from my family put together a special gathering at my house. They organized a fun little shrimp and grits cooking competition, and we all enjoyed ourselves immensely. And not long following that, a big group of us went out together for dinner and a movie to celebrate

Sheryl's and Diane's birthdays. Both of them have a birthday in the same month.

It appeared that things were getting back on track. And it was my thought that things would be smooth for a little while at least. But unfortunately, that wasn't the case. I really wasn't feeling all that well on the day we all went out, but I didn't want to stay home by myself, so I pushed through and went along.

A few days after our outing, I started to feel very strange…like something was wrong with my head. I was seeing things, hearing things, and believing things that weren't true—hallucinations I guess is what you would call them. I didn't want to worry Sheryl too much, but she knew something was wrong. After two days of this, I developed a headache out of this world. I started having double vision and was using words that made absolutely no sense. So, Sheryl decided that she needed to get me to the hospital. She rushed me down to the ER, and they ran tests and took scans of my head. While in the ER, I overheard the doctor tell her that I have a brain bleed and that they only thing they could do is give me some medicine to hopefully make it stop bleeding. But here I am…I haven't been home since.

\*\*\*\*\*

"There you have it, Aurora. That's my story. The good, the bad, and the beautiful. That's everything. Now, I'm just trying to figure out when I'm getting out of here. I really do want to go home."

Aurora asked, "Do you feel as though you're ready to leave?"

"Yes, more than you know."

She smiled and added, "I think I know…"

I noticed that the sun was starting to come up, and after hours of talking while Aurora sat and listened, I was starting to get a little sleepy again. It must've been obvious to her because she told me to rest and she would be back later.

I don't remember seeing my kids or anyone else yesterday. It's weird because I don't think they'd let a day go by without coming to see me. To be honest, it's hard to keep up with days, time, and all that lately. At times, I feel as though I'm out of my body witnessing things happening. I feel so out of sorts. One moment I feel fine, and the next I feel absolutely horrible. I just wish I could go home! I'm so confused about what's really going on with me. And the only time I'm able to communicate is when Aurora is here. These doctors and nurses must be drugging me up something awful during the day.

The shadows cast by the trees outside my window are starting to stretch out long across my room as the sun is rising. I'm lying here in silence with nothing to listen to but my own thoughts. I'll just close my eyes and wait…on what, I don't know. But the way I'm feeling in this the moment, it feels like I'm waiting on the Lord.

It's been a long few minutes of silence, but now I hear foot-steps coming down the hall, and the door opens. My heart is leaping because I smell a familiar perfume that tells me it must be Sheryl. At this point, I can't even open my eyes. I'm so upset with this place. How can they allow these folks to drug me to the point where I can't even interact with anyone during the day? I hear bags shuffling, the TV is turned on. Then I feel Sheryl stroking my arm, and I hear her make a long sigh.

"Huhhhh. Hey, Mama. I'm sorry I'm just getting here. I had a lot to take care of today. I just want you to know that I'm going to be okay. You don't have to worry. I know you worry about me all the time. But, please, know I'm going to be okay. I have all the support in the world. Darryl is here from Phoenix for as long as he can be, and Joshua has been checking in with me every day. Mama, you did a good job raising us. We just want you to know that you're blessed, we're blessed, and all is well. You can rest in knowing everything is okay, and we love you so, so, so much."

What is Sheryl talking about? I know she just had surgery a few months ago, but why does she keep saying she's going to be okay? This is so frustrating. Being able to hear but not being able to respond is torture! I feel her grab my hand and hold on to it while she sits there in silence, the sound of the TV and her sniffling the only sounds in the room. I'm screaming inside because I want to be able to talk to my daughter.

What seems like hours have passed, and the next noise I hear is the door opening again, then I hear my name being called.

"Elizabeth. Elizabeth, it's me Aurora."

I open my eyes and scan the room for Sheryl, but she's gone. I'm alert now, but no one is around except me and Aurora.

"Hey, listen. Can you please find out if my doctor or nurse is available? I'm upset!"

"Tell me what's wrong."

"Well, for one, I feel like they're drugging me too much or something because during the day, I feel like crap, and I can't interact with anyone. My daughter was just here, and I couldn't see her. I couldn't talk to her or anything! I need them to stop giving me whatever it is they're giving me. I can't take it. I want to get out of here!"

She responds in a calm voice, "Elizabeth, you'll be glad to know that your time here is just about over. It's almost time to go home."

"When? When do I leave? Can I leave now?"

"Well, that's up to you. Your time here is up, and you can leave whenever you're ready. Just as your daughter said, your children are going to be okay, and you don't have to worry about—"

"Wait a minute. How do you know what my daughter said earlier? You weren't even here."

She smiles, and a glow radiates from her eyes like nothing I have seen before. It's in that moment that I see her real beauty.

"Elizabeth, I was indeed here when she said that to you, you just couldn't see me."

"What? What do you mean? Help me understand."

"Elizabeth, I have been assigned to you."

"Yes, Aurora. We've already covered that a couple of days ago. I'm trying to understand what you meant when you said—"

She raises her hand, motioning me to stop. "What I'm saying is that I have been on assignment with you from the moment you were manifested on this earth. I must tell you now that I've watched over you every day and every night of your life. Those stories you shared, I was with you through all of that. You've been able to recall those times of the good and bad that you have gone through in life so that you could take inventory of the Most High's goodness, mercy, and love toward you. The Most High has brought you through so much, Elizabeth.

"Oftentimes when a person is transitioning, their life replays in their mind. Yours just so happened to replay as a sequence of nighttime conversations with me. And now, I'm here to comfort you as you make your transition to be with the Most High forever, and that's the point at which my assignment with you will be over."

Aurora's words are ringing in my soul. I understand what she is telling me. She has been my guardian angel, keeping watch over me my entire life. I now understand what's happening to me. I'm leaving this earthly body, and I'm going on to be with the Lord. I understand it all now.

These past few days, I've been reliving a million moments of my life as a playback, allowing me to take inventory and remember all the things I have been blessed to experience within my lifetime, the ups and the downs, everything. They all contributed to the person I am. And it is through these experiences that I have evolved and learned that my life is not just about me. It's about helping someone else along the way.

I have been blessed, and I have been able to be a blessing to others from what God has blessed me with. It's like a ring of never-ending love. And I am so happy that I was a part of the cyclical exchange. Thus, I've never been ashamed to share my story with others because it helps people to see God's grace, mercy, and his preserving power. He has certainly kept me! And through it all, I have come to know that he loves me with an everlasting love, so much so that he gave an angel charge over me. I am overwhelmed with gratitude.

My soul leaps for joy. "Bless the name of the Lord!"

Aurora adds, "Hallelujah!" She reaches for my hand and asks, "Are you ready to go now?"

"Wait, what about my children, my family? And what about Sheryl? She's still not back to work and has to have her last surgery. She's got…"

"Elizabeth, Sheryl will be fine. Do you not know that the Most High has her covered too? She is part of his promise he made to you. And he will fulfill his promise. She is blessed, and she will be just fine. And so shall it be for your sons."

I take hold of Aurora's outstretched hand, and I get up from my bed. I turn around and see my body still lying on the bed. The light from the window glows so bright that it illuminates the entire room. Just as I turn to Aurora, the door to my room opens again, and I see my children come in.

They are all standing around my bed. Sheryl bends over, kisses my forehead, and comments on how cold my forehead is.

I turn back to Aurora. "They know I've passed away, don't they?"

"Yes. They do."

"Can I say anything to them? Will they be able to hear me?"

"They won't be able to hear you, but although you won't be with them physically, they'll be able to feel your love for them. The Most High will give them sweet dreams of you and flashes of memories of your times together that will bring them comfort.

"Come with me, Elizabeth. It's time to go now. Have no fear. Everything is and will be as it should."

In that moment, I realize that my time here is done. I have left a thumbprint on my children, and I have finished my charge. I feel so much peace. This is like nothing I've ever felt before. No more worries, no more heartache, no more pain. Nothing but peace, love, and eternal rest.

And as I begin to follow Aurora, an old gospel hymn my mother used to play on that old out-of-tune piano on Kennerly Street fills my soul. Unspeakable joy fills my heart as I begin to sing.

> Blessed assurance,
> Jesus is mine;
> Oh, what a foretaste of glory divine!
> Heir of salvation, purchase of God
> Born of His Spirit, washed in His blood.
> This is my story, this is my song,
> Praising my Savior all the day long.
> Hmm, hmm, hmm, hmm, hmm…

THE END

# ABOUT THE AUTHOR

Sharon Rowland was born and raised in Detroit, Michigan. She has two older brothers and a large close-knit extended family. While growing up, Sharon often had the opportunity to listen to her mother tell lively stories throughout the years, and they usually occurred during the large family gatherings. This is what sparked Sharon's interest in the art of storytelling. While at Wayne State University as an undergraduate student, she enrolled in an African-American literature class. After receiving encouragement from her instructor, she considered the idea of one day becoming an author. After many years of reading others' literary works, she became more fueled with a desire to create her own work. As a first-time author, Sharon has composed a literary tribute that's rooted in authenticity and inspired by true events taken from her mother's life story.

CPSIA information can be obtained
at www.ICGtesting.com
Printed in the USA
BVHW030833051220
594960BV00011B/233

9 781662 413193